The Knowing

The Knowing

M.D. Lima

A portion of the proceeds from the sale of this book will
be donated to the
American Cancer Society's
Making Strides Against Breast Cancer campaign.

If you'd like to donate directly to their vital work to end
cancer as we know it, for everyone, please visit
www.makingstrideswalk.org
or
https://donate.cancer.org

Dedicated to my amazing family.
No matter how many years we have together,
it will never be enough.

With deepest gratitude to my editor, and dear friend,
Cisa Linxwiler

I have used names of people in my life to name the characters, but the names have absolutely no connection to the persona of the characters they are assigned. I chose them very much at random as I was writing the story, so read nothing into that. Truly.

Dear Reader,

This is not an ordinary book. This is the first piece of a project that you are invited to join. I'd like to thank you for investing in this project – whether that investment be the time you spend reading it, your finances in buying it, or your creative energy in responding to it, sincerely, I thank you.

Book 1 of The Knowing series is intended to lay the foundation for the story and the phenomenon that makes the story possible. It builds the architecture of the narrative, but the deeper narrative and character development are yet to unfold.

Which is where you come in – when you have finished reading Book 1, see the last page for instructions about how to respond. I want YOU to be a part of the story. Share your thoughts and ideas with me. Tell me if you would want to know when you would die, and if so, how would it change the way you live your life? This book project is an interactive experience where you get to help create the story. I hope to weave in as many reader ideas as possible. So, you could see YOUR idea in the next book.

This is unlike any book out there – be a part of it – the adventure, the creation, the unfolding of THE KNOWING.

-M.D. Lima

1.

I must have been about three years old when I first heard the term, The Knowing. Three seems young for such a memory but the recollection is accompanied by the image of my mother's belly swollen with the pending arrival of my little sister, Elizabeth. So I must have been three.

My mother's reaction to the term is what burned the memory into my brain I suppose. She screamed. A shrill howl of utter frustration embroiled with anger and disgust. My mother never screamed. She never even raised her voice. She was a gentle woman who spoke softly and whose touch was even softer than her voice. She was beauty and grace embodied. I adored her. She was my hero.

But that is all I recall. I don't know why she shrieked at the sound of something that is essentially the center of our society. The Knowing. It defines us. We are the Known and the Unknown. That is our way.

It hasn't always been this way. Before The Discovery, no one was Known. My mother believes it was probably better that way. Simpler. More natural. The way life should be. But that's all part of our history now. There is no going back.

The story is told that just a few generations ago, a strange physical manifestation began occurring in five-year-old children of a particular small village. On the morning of their fifth birthdays, the children each developed what appeared to be numerals on the back of their neck, just at the nape. Some children had single digit numerals; others had double. One child even had a triple digit numeral. But he was the only one.

The numerals appeared as though they had been tattooed, but none of the children had done any such thing. No one could explain it, and it had the parents of the village in a frenzy. Was someone terrorizing their children? And how? What did it all mean?

After months of interviews, physical exams, and far more media coverage than they would've preferred, aside from residing in the same village, the one common denominator amongst ALL of the children was that they had been delivered by the same obstetrician. Dr. Matthew Satania.

Dr. Satania, it seems, had a penchant for yanking children from their mother's cervix with a well-worn set of obstetrical forceps. The legend has it that he barely gave the mother a chance to push her baby out before he reached in with his tongs and ripped the child away. In addition to the emotional trauma this undoubtedly caused the parents, the more prominent side effect of this tactic was that with his forceps he had unknowingly (or was it so?) depressed a small section of soft tissue at the base of the child's head, causing each of his deliveries to have the same impression at the back of their skull. Dr. Satania had seemingly created a biological calling card on the body of his patients. It was almost like a small opening, but not quite. More of a dent.

It was from this "dent" that the numerals seemed to flow. As though they had slid right down from the child's brain and onto the back of their neck through that almost like a small opening, but not quite spot.

There were 97 of Dr. Satania's patients in the village who turned five that year. They all bore a numeral. When January of the new year rolled around, parents of then four-year-old Satania patients held their breath in fear. Would their newly turned five-year-olds have the same fate as their predecessors? And what did it all mean? A year had passed, and still, no one could explain anything more than the common factor in Dr. Satania.

January passed and not a single child turning five displayed the numerals. Parents began to relax. This was a good sign. Maybe their children would be untouched by the mysterious mark. Weeks went by, and the world lost interest in the village. Families tried to return to some semblance of normalcy.

Until February 13th. The village broke out in a panic when Rachel Johnson woke up on February 13th, the day of her fifth birthday, with the numeral six on her neck. Her mother let out a wail when Rachel came down the stairs that morning. Rachel broke into such hysteria that she had to be rushed to the hospital and given oxygen. It was three days before her mother could stop crying. She wasn't even certain what she was crying about. But she knew this couldn't be good.

As it turns out, Dr. Satania had been out of the country visiting his family overseas for the entire month of January and the first part of February, five years prior. He didn't deliver any babies in the village during that six-week period. Rachel Johnson was the first delivery he made upon his return to work - February 13th.

2.

By the wee hours of February 14th, the village was under siege. Reporters, government officials, scientists from around the world, and gawkers who wanted to see the Numbered Children, as they called them. By the end of the week, three more children had been numbered, and no one was any closer to understanding why or how this was happening.

Parents would sit anxiously at the bedside of their rising five-year-olds, waiting for their birthday morning sun to rise and reveal their child's fate. Cries could be heard from homes around the village on the morning of many fifth birthdays that year.

Fear ran rampant through the village. Dr. Satania had become a pariah, unable to leave his home. Death threats came in every day as the villagers grew more and more certain that he was to blame for this nightmarish plague on their children. And the longer they went without answers, the more frightened and angrier they became.

Dr. Satania swore that he knew nothing. While he admitted to his proclivity for the use of forceps, he insisted it was because he couldn't bear to see his patients suffer during childbirth, so he hastened the act with a handy set of tongs passed down to him by his med school mentor. He was new to practicing medicine, and very young. The village was his first assignment out of medical school. And though his logic was warped, he seemed sincere and genuinely clueless about the cause of this phenomenon.

Month after month passed with no answers. Dr. Satania closed his practice and returned to his family's home overseas. The threats and the hostility from his community had finally broken him. Government officials insisted he maintain contact with them so they could reach him if any discoveries were made. He agreed and said his goodbyes as he boarded a plane back to his homeland. Perhaps he should've never left home in the first place. Medical school had been such a disaster that this little village is the only place that would hire him. Now he was an exile in his field. He would go home and work in his father's restaurant.

The nightmare continued in his absence. For the next three years, Dr. Satania's babies continued to turn five, and each one continued to bear a numeral marking on his or her neck upon the morning of their fifth birthday. At the end of that third year (five years after the first Numbered Child had been identified), the last of Dr. Satania's Numbered Children turned five on December 31st. The boy woke up with the numeral six on his neck, exactly as Rachel Johnson had done five years prior. It was the first time a single digit numeral had been repeated in more than one child.

That was the first real clue to what would become known as The Discovery. Rachel Johnson, who had manifested the numeral six on her neck, died at the age of six. At the time, no one drew any sort of correlation between the numeral on her neck, and the age of her death. She was tragically killed in a car accident. Her family was too devastated to think of much of anything aside from their grief.

Until Peter Gardener awoke to the same numeral fate. Could it be that simple? Would it be something so morbid? Was the numeral on their neck the age at which they would die? Certainly not. Preposterous. The researchers who had been studying this case since it broke laughed at the very thought. Ridiculous.

Peter Gardener died three months later from a rare form of eye cancer. Only six weeks after he began having severe headaches which were the result of Ocular Melanoma.

Parents of children who bore single digit numerals collapsed into despair. Would their children soon die as well? How could this be? The emotional toll was felt throughout the entire village. Everyone knew a family that was affected by this mystery. No one was untouched.

In the midst of their grief, however, the villagers began to grasp that something good might come from this. With the correlation drawn between the deaths of two Numbered Children, the scientists could now study their remains for more clues. Peter's parents reluctantly agreed to let them study his body. Rachel's family took a great deal of coaxing, but eventually agreed to allow them to unearth her corpse for further study. As agonizing as it was, they hoped the gruesome task might help other families find answers.

3.

Within hours of exhuming Rachel's body, the scientists discovered a biological anomaly in the brains of each of the deceased Numbered Children. Peter's brain was of course much easier to study considering his recent death, but Rachel's corpse was a treasure trove of discoveries despite its decomposition. The clues were still there.

What they found was that the dent made in the child's skull by Dr. Satania's forceps had opened to what appeared to be a tiny cylindrical compartment in the brain. That which felt like a dent from the exterior of the head, was actually more of a tiny lid covering the compartment.

Researchers concluded that the forceps must have broken away a bit of the infant's soft skull tissue during childbirth. Nothing that would be noticeable in an otherwise healthy newborn.

As the child grew it appeared that the soft tissue hardened and healed into place over this area forming a lid. When they removed the lid, a tiny space was revealed – a tube of sorts. It was unlike anything they had seen before in the human brain. A storage compartment that was hidden except for the fact that this deformity created a doorway to the compartment in those children who had been delivered in this manner.

They had what they knew was an important clue, but they had no idea what it meant. Another year passed.

4.

Support groups had formed for the parents of the single digit Numbered Children. Their anxiety was becoming a community issue. It was affecting all facets of village life. They didn't know for sure that their children were soon to die, but the mere suggestion that their numeral might dictate their death age was more than many of these parents could bear. The mental health unit of the village hospital saw a huge uptick in patients suffering from nervous breakdowns. All of them were parents of single-digit Numbered Children. They were cracking from the pressure of anticipating their child's death.

No more children had died, but the next single digit numeral on a Numbered Child was eight, and that child was only seven. The entire village seemed to collectively hold its breath when Chloe Nelson turned eight. Her birthday passed without incident, and everyone breathed a momentary sigh of relief.

In her untamable anxiety, Chloe's mother, Leenie, took every possible precaution to protect her child from any imaginable form of accidental death. Chloe wore any manner of protective gear that her mother could find. The poor child barely left home. Her mother homeschooled her that year to avoid letting her out of her sight.

On the night before her ninth birthday, the village was

bubbling with excitement. If Chloe survived the night, the Numbered Children nightmare might be no more. Maybe the deaths of the first two children were purely coincidental. True, the discovery about their brains was certainly interesting, but that didn't mean all of the children were going to die. They wanted so much for this to be over. Everyone went to sleep that night with hope in their hearts.

In her desperation to protect her child, Chloe's mother crawled into bed beside her so she could keep watch through the night. She fixed her unwavering gaze on her daughter's face like a lion protecting her cub. Her husband awoke to her screams at 1:00 AM when she startled awake to realize she had smothered Chloe in her sleep by inadvertently rolling on top of the child, burying her face in the bed pillows.

Earlier in the evening, having tolerated, but never fully bought into the notion that Chloe was destined to die at age eight, Chloe's father slipped a sleeping pill into his wife's drink at dinner. He had hoped his wife would finally be able to get a bit of rest as she lay next to their precious daughter on this most stressful of all nights. Her anxiety was at maniacal level, and he was afraid she was going to crack from the pressure and lack of sleep.

With the narcotic in her system, Chloe's mother was deeply sedated and never felt or heard a thing. Chloe had slipped away without notice. The coroner judged that she had been dead for approximately two hours. Her death certificate read 11:00 PM. Together, her parents had managed to fulfill her destiny.

The entire village lost its collective mind.

5.

Two more years passed. Every child that had been delivered during Dr. Satania's five-year tenure as an obstetrician had reached their fifth birthday. And every one of them bore a numeral on their neck.

Four more single digit Numbered Children died and two more were nearing what the news media now callously referred to as their "expiration date." None of the single digits had escaped their numeric fate. At this point, it was clear what the numerals meant. But why? And how was it happening?

The years went by and though they never fully fell out of the spotlight, the world grew less interested in the Numbered Children. They went on about their lives, as normally as possible. Many had mental health issues from the strain of knowing when they would die. The anticipation was agonizing and drove several of the now grown children to commit suicide on their fated birthday. Others found solace in drugs and alcohol to numb the constant internal dialogue about their impending date with death. It affected every decision they made. They couldn't escape the gravity of this knowledge. It was too much to carry.

And then there were a few who seemed to embrace the notion that they knew how much time they had and went about their days squeezing life dry of every ounce of joy. Those folks typically ended up with a mountain of debt from their love affair with life (all that high living isn't cheap), but what did they care? They knew they were going to be dead by 29, or 34, or whatever the case may be, so to hell with it. Run up some debt, have a blast and "Sayōnara bitches!"

Fortunately for the credit card companies there were only a few who went down that path. Once they caught on to the scheme, creditors began inquiring about an individual's status as a Numbered Child on the credit application. They wouldn't let that happen again.

Otherwise, the world would mostly forget about that strange Numbered Children story.

Until a Ph.D. student at the village university dug up an article about the phenomenon and decided to write a paper about it. Suddenly, the Numbered Children were causing a stir again.

The student, Olivia Dail, posed a hypothesis that knowing one's time of death would significantly alter the path of one's life. In an effort to prove her hypothesis, she set out to interview the remaining 312 members of the Numbered Children clan. Her ambitious project grabbed the attention of a local reporter, who nudged the story to a national reporter, and suddenly the village was under siege again.

Everyone wanted to return to the scene of the bizarre story about the strangely marked children. Even Dr. Satania (who had not practiced medicine since he went back to his homeland) was dragged in front of a camera. The press tracked him down halfway across the world to interrogate him all these years later.

It was his worst nightmare. He had nearly convinced

himself it was all just a terrible dream. His reality came crashing back as his face again splashed across newspapers and television screens around the world. "Dr. SATAN" they called him. Cartoon images of him with horns and a tail seemed to be everywhere he turned. Someone had even painted a graffiti image of his devilish likeness on the side of his family's home. He was mortified. But there was no escaping it. There was nowhere to hide. They would track him down again. He had to face their cameras and their questions. He packed a bag and boarded a flight to the village.

6.

By the time Dr. Satania (who now preferred to be called Matthew) arrived in the village, emotions were at an all-time high. Villagers were clashing with members of the press who had camped out in every corner of the already bustling town. The few Numbered Children who still lived there (most wanted to get as far away as they could), were being hunted like animals by reporters and freakshow seekers.

Matthew Satania walked into Constable Mark's office and introduced himself. A laughingly unnecessary act considering everyone knew who he was. He was practically a walking, talking ghost story. Children still giggled with delight at scary stories about "Dr. Satan who yanked babies from their mommies!" He read the room and sat down sheepishly in a chair in the corner.

All of the village leaders were gathered in the room. Some looking nervous and fussy, others looking exhausted and strung out. But none of them looked happy. Only a few of those present were old enough to be involved in the original fiasco of the Numbered Children, but everyone knew the story by heart. It had unfortunately become a defining factor of their local history.

No one quite knew how to begin the meeting that seemed to have called itself. Constable Mark, who had in fact been a young officer of the law when this story first unfolded, stood at the front of the room and asked if anyone had any ideas about how they should handle the hysteria at hand.

The room erupted in shouts and hollers, guffaws and laughter. There might have even been a snort or a fart in there somewhere. But no one had a viable answer about how to handle the mania that was just outside the front door of the Great Hall where they met.

Constable Mark shouted for silence in the room. The room settled. "We have to get to the bottom of this craziness," he began. "We have to tell these people something more than the NOTHING we've been telling them all these years! Dr. Satania, I mean, Matthew, have you learned ANYTHING more in all these years that could help us?" His voice was on the edge of pleading as he turned to Matthew.

Matthew stared and his shoes and shook his head. He had put this all behind him years ago. He had tried NOT to think about it. He certainly had not continued researching it.

"Say something, you MONSTER!" came a shout from the back of the room. Matthew sprang to his feet, surprising himself. "I am NOT a MONSTER!" he screamed, tears welling up in his eyes. "I did NOTHING to intentionally hurt anyone. I just want all of this to be over."

"Well, as you can see," Constable Mark pointed to the crowd outside the window overlooking the square, "this isn't going anywhere anytime soon, so I suggest you help us find our way out of it."

With a heavy sigh, Matthew dragged a chair to the giant conference table at the center of the room and motioned for everyone to do the same. After a few moments of shuffling and chairs sliding across the parquet flooring, everyone was seated and at attention.

Matthew bowed his head for a moment, took a deep breath, and said, "Okay, let's begin."

Over the course of several hours that evening, the assembly of men (yes, of course it was a bunch of men) decided to find a way to turn what had been a traumatic past into their finest asset. They had to find a way to push it through the public psyche by making them believe it was a blessing, not a curse. They would set out on the greatest marketing campaign since Christianity. They were going to harness this Numeric Nightmare into a must have fashion statement.

The first order of business was to convince those most deeply affected by this enigma that it wasn't an altogether bad thing. These were the people who had been living this nightmare for years – it wasn't going to be a simple mission. Constable Mark called a meeting of the Numbered Children and their families.

The room was packed wall to wall. Parents, grandparents, siblings, spouses and yes, the Numbered Children themselves, filled the room. There wasn't an empty seat and the tension in the room was stifling. Hundreds of distrusting eyes stared at Constable Mark as he approached the podium.

Constable Mark began by telling the crowd that they all had a remarkable opportunity at hand. He framed the new swarm of attention as a chance to garner support for advanced research into the case of the Numbered Children, and possibly find some sense of closure for all those affected. Distrusting eyes continued to burn through him.

Eternally the wordsmith, Constable Mark wove a tale for his listeners that spoke of vindication for the Numbered Children who had spent much of their lives under the heartless microscope of the media. He even spoke of possible financial reparations for the families affected.

The mention of money had some of the crowd reacting a bit more favorably. Their hardships could certainly stand a bit of financial gain. But he could see that not everyone was so receptive. No amount of money could take away the pain they had endured. So, he changed gears a bit to appeal to their egos.

He talked about how they would all be heroes if scientists could take what they might learn from studying this phenomenon and turn it into some sort of scientific advance rather than a freakshow. The Numbered Children could be pioneers of a new frontier, he crooned. The crowd was not convinced.

A man at the back of the room stood abruptly and stormed out of the assembly hall. The door slammed behind him. The man's wife scurried out after him, tears in her eyes. The couple had recently lost their daughter, Donna, to her numeric providence. Donna was marked with the numeral 27. As fate would have it, she had discovered her pregnancy only days before she was killed by a stray bullet in a drive by shooting. The sting of losing their daughter and unborn granddaughter was simply too much. It was too soon.

Constable Mark cleared his throat nervously and opened his mouth to continue his sales pitch when an older, well-dressed woman stood and shouted over the crowd, "Will we allow all of this to be for nothing? Look at the pain you've all known from carrying this knowledge of their death year...we became so consumed with their death that many of us forgot how to live. This cannot be in vain. My son, Jeremiah, died at 22, just as we knew he would. The first few years of knowing his fate nearly ate us alive. But then we chose to embrace his destiny rather than fear it. And our lives changed in every way. We spent the years we had with Jeremiah LIVING rather than mourning. And it was absolutely magical. I miss him every day, but I am so grateful that I was able to soak up every beautiful moment I had with him. Knowing how much time he had changed everything. We're all going to die. There's no escaping that. But by knowing how long we had together, we spent every day focused on what was truly important to us. We've all heard the phrase, 'Live like you're dying.' Our family actually did that, and it was the greatest gift I have ever received." She straightened her spine and turned to face Constable Mark directly, "I would be willing to allow you to study my son's remains if it will help further the understanding of what we've all been through, and in the hope that something good can come from it for future generations."

The room fell silent. The conviction in her voice was so raw and powerful that even Constable Mark was deeply moved. He realized he had lost himself in her monologue and shook his head to clear his mind and find his way back to the task at hand. As the woman took her seat, Constable Mark uttered only two words, "Thank you." She had just done his job for him.

The next morning, the first thing Constable Mark said to the press was this: "Picture a world where you can plan out every moment of your life...because you know just how many moments you have!"

The room full of reporters was abnormally silent. A few members of the media shifted uncomfortably in their seats and looked around the room to gauge the reaction of their cohorts. No one understood where he was going with this. Was he serious?

Constable Mark continued, painting a picture of a society where people could CHOOSE to find out what year they would die so they could use that information to plan their lives to the moment. "Think of the efficiency, the motivation to live fully, the ability to choose one's path based on one's known finish," he lavished. He painted a picture of a world where uncertainty and worry could be abated because we'd already know how, or at least when, our story ends.

Eyes of distrust turned into looks of curiosity which turned into hushed whispers around the room. They were soaking it up. They were actually discussing it. Albeit quietly and with much guarded voices, but they were discussing it. Constable Mark looked across the room at Matthew, who was taking it all in from the back wall. Matthew's eyebrows raised. Maybe they were onto something.

7.

The next morning a call came in from the Prime Minister's office. Constable Mark nearly choked on his breakfast biscuit when the receptionist buzzed the call through to his phone.

The Prime Minister, it seemed, had been following the story of the Numbered Children since its inception. This new resurgence of the story fascinated him, and he wanted to know more. Constable Mark knew this was his moment. He painted for the Prime Minister the same utopian portrait that he had shared with the press. Prime Minister Blanchman hung on every word. He was hooked.

The concept of knowing one's ultimate finish intrigued the PM both personally and politically. Think of the implications it could have on his ability to support (read: control) the citizenry with this sort of information at his disposal. Resources could be expended more wisely on those who were around for the long haul, with the short termers getting only what they need to survive. Why waste the money on them when we knew they wouldn't be around long? The triple digit numbers could be groomed to maintain the proper world order for years to come. They would be given positions of leadership. Of course, none of this passed through his lips and over the phone line, but his mind raced with possibilities.

As soon as he hung up the phone, Constable Mark called

Matthew to tell him the good news. They were on their way to greatness.

The PM immediately summoned his Health Ministry and discussed the possibility with them, painting the same rosy portrait that Constable Mark had painted for him on the phone. At first the room of doctors and scientists fell silent, just as it did with the press. But much like the members of the media, the room full of health professionals found themselves strangely intrigued. There were a few voices who spoke up with ethical concerns about the prospect, but the snarls and sneers from their peers quieted them quickly. This was not a heroic bunch. The dissenters buried their heads and quickly toed the line. The power that could come from being the nation to launch this scientific bombshell was more enticing than any of them could stand.

And so, it was settled. The Health Ministry would invest a sizable sum into the research of the Numbered Children project in hopes that it would become an amazing prospect for all citizens (and an amazing opportunity for the govern- ment to enhance [read: control] the lives of its people). A chance to map out one's entire life with a real sense of purpose from knowing how much time we have. A gift to the people is how they would sell it.

There was just one problem...before they could give that gift they had to figure out how to replicate it.

8.

Constable Mark knew he and Matthew Satania had their work cut out for them. They had to figure out how to dependably recreate the effect. The money rolling in from the health ministry certainly made the task more feasible, but there were so many things that could go wrong. Fortunately, Sandra Zagursky's emotional speech at the recent meeting had inspired others to agree to let the researchers examine the remains of their deceased Numbered Child. The more research samples they could attain, the better chance they had of reverse engineering the numeral effect. So far, they had seven bodies to study, in addition to the two they had researched years before. It was time to get to work.

The seven corpses, in varying degrees of decomposition, were arranged on seven tables across the university laboratory where Matthew had set up his operations. The two original specimens were preserved in the local morgue and would be joining their comrades later that day when the paperwork was complete. They were still awaiting a few signatures from local authorities.

Matthew stood silently at the front of the room staring at the neatly arranged bodies of his former patients. He had once held their newborn bodies in the palm of his hand. And by doing so, he had ruined their lives. Or had he? Maybe this had indeed been a gift. He thought back to Sandra's powerful words…maybe they had lived lives that would never have been possible without the knowledge he had allowed them. With that knowledge better understood and properly harnessed, everyone could live life in absolute fullness. This gift could change the world. He would be a hero. And he would be vindicated. Finally.

He pulled back the sheet on the corpse of Danika Harrison and sliced open the posterior of her skull. For the first time in ages, he smiled. By the end of that day, he had been able to locate the dent, known now as the Keyall, on each of the seven specimens. Each Keyall was identical to the others except one. The Keyall in the brain of Elliott Call had microscopic remnants of a black substance that he had not found in the others. Upon further examination, the remnants were found to be an ink-like substance, much like that found in an octopus. This was a huge break, and though he had been working feverishly for nearly 15 hours, day one had been an enormous success.

Matthew shot up in bed at the sound of his phone ringing just beside his head on the nightstand of his hotel room. The village had only one hotel when he lived here years ago, but thanks to his legacy, the village now boasted 12 hotels to meet the demand of the tourism industry that had been the product of the Numbered Children.

It was Constable Mark. He was breathing heavily. "Come quickly!" he huffed. Matthew could tell Constable Mark was running while he talked. And he wasn't exactly the fittest of the fit. "Lorelei James just dropped dead, and her body is headed to the morgue as we speak. Her family gave us permission to use her remains – you have to get here NOW and begin your exam. You'll probably never have the opportunity to examine a corpse as fresh as this one! Get over here NOW!" Matthew winced at the insensitive nature of Constable Mark's words. "Fresh" was not a word one would ordinarily want to use when referring to a recently deceased human being, but he was right. This was an extraordinary opportunity to examine a body as close to alive as possible (at least for now).

Matthew grabbed his crumpled jeans from the floor, hopped on one foot to dress himself as he crossed the room to reach his shoes and was out the door in moments. When he arrived at the morgue, the technicians had already prepared Lorelei's body on the table for him to examine. She had been dead for just over two hours, so her body was still slightly warm and flaccid, but he didn't have much time. Within the hour she would begin to stiffen and chemical changes in her fibers would begin. He needed to examine her before the Keyall might be altered in some way. He picked up his scalpel and began.

He had only been working for a matter of moments when he gasped and his hands stopped. "Someone bring me a camera, please! Quickly!" One of the technicians handed him the instant camera they had for morgue use and he leaned closely and took several pictures of the area. Suddenly he screamed, "Oh no, what's happening?!" As he stared helplessly, the area he had just photographed began to change. The tiny vein he had examined was shrinking and ultimately disappeared completely. He waited anxiously as the instant film reached full exposure and the photos were revealed. What the images showed, but was no longer visible on Lorelei's corpse was a tiny capillary like vein running from the base of the Keyall down toward the back of the neck. It was the delivery system. The ink substance was released from the Keyall on the 5th birthday (why then? So many questions still to be answered). It travelled down these tiny capillaries to the nape where the ink was dispensed in the form of a numeral.

Matthew grabbed his scalpel and sliced down the back of the neck, peeling back the skin. As the skin pulled away from the tissue beneath, hundreds of tiny veins were revealed that terminated at the dermis layer of her skin. They were spread across the nape of her neck like little pinheads forming a distinct shape. The shape of two numerals. Two and nine. Today was Lorelei's 29th birthday.

A few hours earlier she had been playing football in the backyard with her brothers at her birthday dinner. Her baby brother tripped and careened into her as he went for a catch. The hard hit to her chest caused sudden cardiac death, also known as commotio cordis. She had never had heart problems. She was dead before she hit the ground.

Her family was one of those that had chosen to embrace every moment they had with their precious daughter, and she had made them promise that they would get her body to Dr. Satania immediately so she could help others like her. Her giving heart may have stopped beating, but it had not stopped giving.

To honor Lorelei's wishes, as soon as she was gone their first call was to Constable Mark. In doing so, she had just helped them answer the HOW it was happening. This was the delivery system for the numerals. It was as though the children were being tattooed from the inside with the resulting image showing on the exterior. A superhighway of capillaries that delivered bursts of the ink substance from beneath the skin formed the shape of one, two or three numerals on the nape. In her case, the numerals 2 and 9.

Within seconds of revealing the delivery system, it was gone. Just as the tiny vessel beneath the Keyall had shriveled away, so too did this intricate tangle. Right before their eyes...gone. And they had not photographed it.

"Dammit!" Matthew screamed. "We lost it!"

"Grab a pencil!" Constable Mark yelled. "Everyone, grab a pencil and write down everything you remember about what we saw. Quickly, while it's still new in your minds!"

It sounded crazy, but no one had a better idea, so they did as he said, quietly scribbling and nodding their heads back and forth as if to literally toss the memories around in their brains. When it was clear everyone was finished, they gathered around Lorelei's corpse once again and pulled the sheet over her head, each man clutching the drawing he created from memory.

"This stays in this room!" Constable Mark demanded. "Do you understand me? One damn word leaves this room and I will personally kick your ass!" They were all in shock. In all the years they had known the Constable, they had NEVER heard him swear before. He was a righteous man and very careful to protect his reputation. They all nodded emphatically.

"He's right," Matthew said. "This is very big, but I don't know yet EXACTLY what it means. I need time to study it further. We CANNOT let this information get out. Got it?"

Everyone nodded again and handed their drawings to Matthew. Constable Mark sent them on their way with, "Okay, then. Get out of here. All of you."

When he was sure they were all well gone, he turned back to Matthew. "What does it mean, Matthew?"

"I'm not entirely sure yet," he said with a sly grin, "but I think it's good news...extremely good news. And it's Dr. Satania."

9.

Matthew, or rather, Dr. Satania, didn't sleep a bit that night. He was facing the wee hours of the morning when he got back to his hotel room. Too early to head to the lab on campus and begin working. University Security would get their bloomers in a bind over that. So he sat down at the writing desk and began making notes about what he had seen. He sketched, and scribbled notes, and hashed out ideas and hypotheses. This went on for three hours until the sun came up. Security couldn't balk now. It was officially morning. He would just be an early bird on campus today.

As he turned the corner to head toward his building, he noticed a young woman sitting on the front steps. The sun was barely over the horizon and this woman, this very pregnant woman, had been sitting on the steps of his building for quite some time. She perked up when she saw him in the distance, and tried mightily to get to her feet, but just as she began to rise, she was stricken with pain, and fell back to the steps with a thud. She cried out.

Dr. Satania sprinted across the lawn toward the woman. She was in labor. Freaking hell. This woman was about to have a baby right here on the front steps of Cecil Hall. As he reached the young woman, she cried out again. Freaking hell. Her contractions were getting closer together. She was breathing heavily.

"I want you to," she gasped in pain, "deliver my baby," she gasped again. And then a gush of fluid from between her legs. Her water broke. Freaking hell. Dr. Satania fumbled for his keys to open the building. He had to get her inside. He propped the door open and went to get the now hyperventilating young woman. He tried to talk her through the anxiety and she was able to slow her breathing a bit. He slowly helped her to her feet and they inched their way to the door.

He had no idea he could ever be so happy to see a lobby couch as he was at that moment. He got the woman to the couch and propped her up as best he could. "I'll be right back," he promised the frantic young woman. "I have to get my instruments. I'll be RIGHT BACK!" He tore off down the hall and jammed a key into the door of the office they had given him when he agreed to stay and help with the research. The young woman could hear him tearing apart the room searching for his tools, cursing continuously as he went.

"Yes!" he cried, and he came tearing back down the hallway with a black bag in one hand and a wad of t-shirts under his other arm. He motioned to the t-shirts: "Best I can do in a pinch", there had been a box of t-shirts left in the office closet from its previous occupant. The shirts were all hot pink and read, "Check Your Humps For Lumps" with an image of a camel with breasts in the place of its humps. The young woman tried to smile, but winced in pain instead.

"Yes, of course! Let's get to work!" Dr. Satania knelt down beside the young woman and opened his black medical bag. He packed it into his suitcase when he left his homeland, knowing there was a very real chance he would need it again, but never did he expect it to be so soon.

First, he removed his stethoscope and set it aside. He wouldn't be needing that quite yet. Then he removed the forceps. Yes, THE forceps that he had used all those years before. The very ones that created the cranial deformity that had become the greatest scientific mystery of his time. The young woman saw the forceps, "Please! Take the baby now so we can know how much life he has to live. Make him a Numbered Child!" she begged as she winced again in pain. Her contractions were getting closer and closer. It wouldn't be long now.

The woman grabbed Dr. Satania by the arm, "Will you do it? Will you deliver my baby the way you did all those other children? Please!" He was shocked. He didn't know how to respond. Here was a woman begging him to perform the very procedure that had ruined his life, and that he thought had ruined the lives of all of those poor people. But she WANTED her child to know his numeric fate. She had been sitting on the steps of this building for hours, in labor, waiting for him to arrive so he could intentionally cause a deformity in her child that would predict the year of his death. He stared at her in disbelief. And then he nodded. She fell back onto the couch with a heavy sigh and a bit of temporary relief from the pain. But it was short lived. Her contractions were now three minutes apart. It was time. He lifted his forceps and delivered her baby just as he had done time and again so many years ago. It was, as they say, like riding a bike.

Later that day as Dr. Satania replayed the morning's episode in his mind, he realized he could not have PLANNED a better publicity event. Students and faculty began arriving at the building just moments after he delivered baby boy, Dakota Winters. The press arrived before the ambulance did. Dakota Winters would forever be known as the literal Birthchild of The Discovery, as he was the first infant delivered in the new era of The Discovery.

The young woman, Dakota's mother, was Laurin Winters. She was a member of a group that absolutely boggled Matthew's mind as she described it – they were something like a cult, but maybe more like a colony. Or perhaps it was a full-blown cult. He couldn't be sure, but clearly it was a group of people living in community because they WANTED to number their children. They had already been trying to replicate Satania's technique for the last five years, but had no success. In fact, there had been nineteen babies delivered using failed attempts at his method. Two of the children had severely misshapen heads as a result of the failed attempts. The remaining seventeen seemed to be mostly okay. So far. The first few had reached their fifth birthday with no markings revealed. Their attempts had failed. The community was on the verge of collapse when one of the members saw an article entitled, "The World Returns to the Village of the Numbered Children." They knew this was a sign. This was precisely the boost they needed.

She went on to tell him that there were several women in her group at various stages of pregnancy, all of whom wanted to have their babies using the Satania Induction Method. He had a method? Woah. Wild. He had a cult following. Literally.

This was better than anything he could have ever imagined. He would be able to immediately utilize the technique to deliver these children and begin an entirely new test group of Numbered Children subjects. It would have taken years to get approval for a scientific study like this, and it would have been far too restrictive to achieve the level of saturation he needed to make the Satania Induction Method a go. Satania Induction Method. He liked the way it felt on his tongue and he snorted at himself when he realized how much he was enjoying this new found attention. Admiration, that is. He'd gotten plenty of attention before, but not the kind he wanted. This. This was a damn good feeling, and he wanted more of it.

10.

The decision was made that Constable Mark would maintain their daily administrative operations at the university while Dr. Satania would go with Laurin to meet the members of her community. They called themselves The Unknown. They considered Numbered Children to be The Known. Though they would never be able to know the schedule of their own fate, they wanted it for their children. Very much. So much so that they had all abandoned the conventional lives they were previously living and come together on a plot of land about 20 miles from the village. They wanted to be close to the original Numbered Children village, but not so close that they drew attention to themselves. They feared the government would step in and try to stop them, so they kept their lifestyle hidden. Until now.

With the Health Ministry funding Dr. Satania's new research, and the media gobbling up every word they could find about the possibility of more Numbered Children in the future, they knew this was their time to step into the light. But they were being far too slow about it, in Laurin Winters' opinion, and she didn't have time to wait around on them. She took matters into her own hands and found Dr. Satania for herself. And her plan had unfolded exactly as she'd hoped. Well, aside from the part where she was stuck lying on the cold brick steps of his office for two hours. That was not exactly what she had imagined, but it was a means to an end. And it worked. By golly, it worked. She would have her Numbered Child.

When Laurin and Dr. Satania entered the encampment of The Unknown, a hush fell over the place. Eyes turned to stare at them from every angle, and there was more than one gasp heard around the camp. It was him. THE Dr. Satania was standing before them, and Laurin stood at his side, beaming proudly with her newborn bundle wrapped in her arms. "He did it!" she shouted gleefully. "He delivered baby Dakota, and now he will be a Numbered Child!" She was giddy with delight. The gathered crowd cheered. Some of the women began to weep...many from the joy of the moment...some from sheer jealousy. Their babies had already been born and would never be included among the Numbered Children. As far as was known at the time, there was no other way to initiate the Numbered Child phenomenon other than by using Dr. Satania's method at birth. They would forever carry their bitterness. It was too late for their babies. Two of the mothers were filled with jealous rage. Rather than bearing the numerals of their fate, their babies would forever bear the mark of a failed attempt at becoming a Numbered Child. They were disgraced mothers whose children would be known as the freaks with the misshapen heads. One of the mothers, Christy Moreland, was so furious that she spit on the ground and stormed away. Her absolute indignation erupted in every angry step she took as she disappeared in the direction of her tiny, makeshift home. She would pack up her family and leave the camp the next morning. She wanted no part of this anymore.

Dr. Satania watched her dramatic exit with concern. Dissenters were bad for the cause. He would need to deal with her later. When Christy was no longer in sight, everyone turned back to face Dr. Satania who smiled nervously and thanked them all for their warm welcome, all but Christy Moreland, that is. That one could drop dead for all he cared. In fact, it would be rather helpful if she did. (He would have to tuck away that thought. At least for now. He could revisit it later.)

He was shaken from his thought when he heard, "I'm next!" squealed by a young red head who waddled up to the front of the group with a pregnant belly so engorged that it looked like it would be difficult to breathe. She was ready to pop at any minute. Dr. Satania smiled and extended his hand for her to shake. Instead, she grabbed him and struggled to wrap her arms around him awkwardly for the giant tummy in her way and gave him the closest thing to a hug that she could muster. She squealed again as she took a step back. She was fangirling over an obstetrician. What in the world was going on? He felt like he had tumbled into an alternate universe. Where were the haters and the death threats now? These people worshipped him. He was a god. And this was only the beginning.

When he returned to the village a week later, he had delivered two more babies at the colony of The Unknown and had spent hours teaching the precise details of the Santania Induction Method to the colony's medical team, comprised of four individuals. In their lives before joining The Unknown, two had been doctors, one was formerly a nurse, and one was an EMT. He felt confident that they had studied carefully and were ready to perform the deliveries after he departed. And he was only 20 miles away. He could return if necessary.

A week later he received a call that the medical team had delivered a baby using his technique and they felt confident that this time it was a success. Unfortunately, there was no way to know for sure until the child reached her fifth birthday, but they were hopeful. They had done everything exactly as he had taught them.

By now word had gotten out about the colony of The Unknown, and they were beginning to feel the pressure of the media's presence. Their private compound in the woods was private no more. Reporters reached their remote location by foot, on four wheelers, and one even hovered in a helicopter above. The members of the colony were not amused. Something had to be done.

They called Dr. Satania. His advice was for them to come out of hiding completely and proudly rejoin society. The concept of having the option to be a member of the Numbered Children was gaining more and more popularity. Family members, like Sandra Zagursky, had begun speaking out in support of the procedure and sharing stories of the beautiful life her child was able to lead because they knew how much time they had with him. She, and those like her, sold the idea to society with passion and the kind of emotion only a mother could marshal. Inquiries about becoming a Numbered Child were flooding in every day. It was time for the people of The Unknown colony to step out and sing the praises of the Numbered Children for all the world to hear.

Meanwhile, the original Numbered Children weren't so

sure. The rosy world being painted by officials was hardly the life any of them had lived. Sure, there had been a few out of the bunch who had bucked the norm and lived wild and free. It sounded great. But society would collapse if everyone followed that path.

11.

Spring term had recently ended at the University so students left campus and returned to their home villages for the summer. As a result, the University dormitories were vacant. Dr. Satania, supported by some very strong words of encouragement (read: threats) from Constable Mark, was able to convince the University administration to let the members of The Unknown colony stay in the dorms temporarily. But only temporarily. Students would be back in a few months. The colonists would need to be long gone by that time.

Dr. Satania didn't know what he was going to do with all of these people, but he knew he needed to bring them out where the world could see them. They could be a model community for the Numbered Children project. A living, breathing, model community where he could test best practices and theories and show the world the kind of success they could enjoy if they joined the movement. Yes, he liked that. The movement to help people live their lives with fullness and purpose. Never a moment wasted. Each one accounted for and applied to its finest use for maximum output. They would be a nation of near demigods, controlling their destiny in a way never possible before. His skin prickled at the thought of it. The power. They would be unstoppable. But first he had to figure out what to do with them at the end of the summer. World domination would have to wait for now.

He picked up his phone and dialed the Prime Minister directly. They had become quite chummy through this whole process of creating a new social movement, and Dr. Satania knew he was going to need to call in another favor.

"Blanch," he said rather casually to Prime Minister Blanch-man who picked up on the other end of the line. "It's Satan," he and the PM had decided it was comical to refer to Matthew with the very term the world had tried to use to torture him. Now he embraced it. A couple of naughty schoolboys on the playground they were. They both snorted at the sound of the word, Satan. It sent chills of delight down the Prime Minister's spine. It felt so dark and primitive.

"I have to put these cult, I mean, colony people somewhere before the summer is out. I need to find a place for them to set up a proper village and show outsiders what a spectacular future we could have if every child was numbered."

The PM chewed his lower lip, "Hmmmm." Dr Satania could practically hear the PM thinking on the other end of the line. His mind flying through the mountains of political favors he could call in to help them solve this problem. "I know exactly what we'll do," he purred. "There is a district about 150 miles west of here. It's fairly remote. A contractor from the far North came down and started building a hous-ing community for the wealthy. He thought he would make it big by creating a resort type retreat, exclusively for the rich. A lovely idea," the Prime Minister said woefully. "Unfortu-nately, he ran out of money before it could be finished. It's been sitting there wasting away for over a year. It will need a lot of repair work, and there are quite a few homes that weren't even finished, but it could be a start. We could even come off as social heroes for helping these families find homes AND rebuilding a community in ruin. It's a win – win," he said coyly. "We win, and we win."

And so, it began. The community would be called Collentacht and it would be founded by a group of brave citizens setting out on a new frontier. A new social order. They would go before the rest of us and pave the way for the lives we deserve. The entire world would be watching.

At the announcement of The Unknown colony's departure, the original Numbered Children were relieved. The presence of this new faction was causing more disruption than anyone needed so they were glad to see them go. Until they realized where they were going.

A few of the now grown original Numbered Children were gathered at a coffee shop on the village square chatting about the recent insanity. "Have you seen this Collentacht place where those cult people are going? It's a paradise," said 28-year-old Grant James. Grant had been one of the Numbered Children who had struggled with drug abuse to dull the voices that wouldn't quiet in his head. Life had not been easy for him. He couldn't help but be jealous that this group of "pioneers" was getting the royal treatment when they had been treated like a circus act. He passed around the photo he'd printed from an article online of the now abandoned resort community. "It looks like a run-down heap of junk to me," one of the young women remarked. "Well, it's been sitting there rotting away for a while, but the bones are good. I mean, really, really good. These homes are mini mansions,"

Grant continued. "And some of them not even so mini. I'm barely surviving, and these kids are being handed the keys to the kingdom. It's not right." His voice was bitter from years of feeling like an outcast. The Numbered Children belonged nowhere and to no one. They were outsiders in every way. And now this group of Numbered Children 2.0 were being hailed as pioneers. Heroes even. It made his blood boil. When the photo came back around the table to Grant, he took one more look at the lavish grounds and grandiose homes before he crumpled it into a ball and threw it on the ground with a growl. He wanted HIS piece of the pie.

"Calm down, Grant," Kimberly tried to comfort him. She'd always had a soft spot for Grant. Nothing ever seemed to go his way. He was a sweet guy with terrible luck. "The sooner these people are gone, the better. Who cares where they go?"

"I care," Grant grumbled as he pushed his chair straight back from the table, hopped to his feet and headed straight out the door of the coffee shop. "That dude has got anger issues," quipped one of the guys at the other end of the table. "Leave him alone. He's been through a lot," Kim defended Grant. She always did. "We've ALL been through a lot," the guy mouthed back. She threw a fork at him and stuck out her tongue.

They didn't always get along, but this group of Numbered Children had been through a lot together. And all they had was each other. No one else could understand what life had been like for them. Even their families couldn't truly relate. It was a lot to carry, especially when they were younger. High school had been a horror story for most of them. As if teenage hormones weren't bad enough...throw in the curse of knowing when you were going to die, and it makes for an emotional tidal wave. Especially if you had a low number. The pressure was unbearable. Many of the girls had found ways to conceal their numerals under their long hair or beneath a scarf. It was a bit harder for the guys to hide their marking with their shorter haircuts and low collars. It was there for everyone to see. And no one ever let them forget. It was always very clear that the Numbered Children were outsiders. No one wanted anything to do with those freakshow kids. They were cursed, and no one wanted to take the chance that the curse was contagious. The fact that the new kids were going to be treated like celebrities was maddening, even for those who didn't outwardly admit it. Their lives had been so unfair. Many of them wondered why would anyone WANT this life for their children? It made no sense at all.

12.

As soon as their travel arrangements were made, The Unknown colony members were anxious to pack their things and make a new start in Collentacht. They knew nothing about their new home, but the last few years had been difficult living rough in their hidden woodland encampment, and even these last few months of piling into university dorms had been less than comfortable. They were looking forward to living in real houses again. They had been in hiding for far too long. Some of the youngest children who had been born at the encampment had never seen indoor plumbing or heat until they arrived at the University dorms. They would be fascinated with the notion of having an entire home of their very own. And now that Dr. Satania had instructed them on how to properly perform his delivery technique, they would surely be reaping the rewards of their die-hard commitment to this movement.

The years passed as the Collentacht community was rebuilt and ultimately became a highly sought after destination. Residents maintained gorgeous homes on perfectly manicured lawns and the area offered luxurious accommodations to those who wanted to escape to the oasis for the weekend or a bit longer. Out-of-town visitors were often more interested in sightseeing the local residents, who had become well known all over the world for the social experiment at which they were the center, than they ever were of the local sights. An entire village of people who had rejected normal society and instead chosen to pursue a completely new order of things – it was fascinating. But there was no denying that the local sights were truly luxurious, and the Collentacht community was nicer than any community built for the rest of the citizenry. And people were starting to talk.

Dakota Winters was now four years old. He would be the first of the Collentacht Numbered Children, now known as the Pioneer Children. The PM felt like the former nomenclature wasn't as flattering as he would like. They needed to have a name that brought hope for the future. The members of the cult formerly known as The Unknown had embraced the new name, but still used the terms known and unknown to differentiate between those who would be marked and those who were not.

Dakota would turn five in two weeks. The Collentacht community could barely stand the wait. They prepared for his day as though he was about to be coronated. He was the embodiment of everything they believed – knowing the approximate date of the end of one's life would change everything about how they lived that life. They would command their own destiny.

The morning of Dakota's fifth birthday arrived. There were throngs of people waiting on the street in front of the Winters home that morning before the sun came up. Even the press had come in for the occasion. Everyone wanted to know how long the first Pioneer Child would have. Would he be a single digit? Would he be around for another century with a triple digit? The wait was nearly over.

Dakota's mother, Laurin, the feisty young woman who had labored on the office building steps for hours waiting for Dr. Satania to arrive that fateful day five years ago, had barely slept a wink all night. Her child was the first of a new generation. She beamed with pride as she tiptoed into his room, just before sunrise.

"Good morning, precious boy," she whispered softly into his tiny ear. "Rise and shine birthday boy." At that, his eyes popped open, and he sat upright.

"What is it? Tell me momma! What's my numeral?" Even at such a young age, Dakota knew this was a big day. He didn't fully understand what it meant that today was the day of his Knowing but everyone seemed very excited, so he was as well.

His mother brushed his hair away from his neck and pulled down the collar of his pajama shirt.

88.

Her baby was going to live a good, long life. Tears welled up in her eyes.

"What is it?" he demanded. "What does it say?" He was sounding panicky at her silence, so she gathered herself and said, "88 my sweet boy. It says 88."

"What does it mean?" he begged her for more. He wanted to understand.

"It means you are going to live a very long life. We have lots of time together."

Dakota smiled at the thought of many years with his mother. He loved her and wanted to stay with her forever.

As the sun came over the horizon, the crowd outside started to grow impatient.

"Come out and show us!" they cried from the street.

Dakota hopped out of bed. He knew they were waiting for him. He felt like a superhero. He ran to the front door. Laurin hurried along behind him. Laurin wrapped her robe tightly around her and opened the front door. The crowd on the street cheered at the sight of the young boy and his mother.

She pushed open the glass storm door and they stepped out onto the front porch.

"Tell us, already!" came a voice from the crowd. They were anxious and impatient. This was such a big day.

Laurin wrapped her arm around her child and they stepped forward a bit, she nudged Dakota to turn around and she lifted his hair from his neck.

"88," she yelled to the crowd trying to speak above the noise as she revealed his markings. There was a split second of silence as they processed what she had told them and then the crowd erupted in hoops and hollers, screams and cries.

88! He would live a long life! This was wonderful news. Just as they had hoped.

Over the next week, the two additional babies that Dr. Satania had delivered for them turned five and each displayed numerals, just as they'd hoped. Timothy Griffin woke to a 67 and Savannah Grey bore the numeral 102. Timothy would have a respectable length of time – he could have a good life. Savannah would be tapped for leadership. Anyone who would be around that long would need to be carefully groomed to maintain our societal order, as it should be.

There were now three Known children in the Collentacht community. Excitement was growing. In just over a week, the next Pioneer Child would turn five. Hannah Crockett was the first baby the community's small medical team had delivered on their own after learning the proper technique from Dr. Satania. Her Knowing would be another step in the right direction toward a new societal norm.

When the day arrived, the scene was repeated on the street in front of the Crockett home. The crowd waited as the sun rose, but no one came through the front door. They waited a few more minutes, chatting and speculating. This went on for nearly an hour when the front door finally opened. The crowd cheered, just as they had done when Dakota emerged only weeks before. But Hannah was not there. And neither was her mother. Instead, Hannah's father, Bill Crockett, stepped onto the porch. His body language did not read celebration.

"There is no marking," he said to the crowd. His voice broke as he continued, "Hannah is not a member of the Pioneer Children. Her Knowing has been a failure."

The energy of the crowd deflated in an instant. What was he saying? How could this be? They had done exactly as Dr. Satania had taught them when Hannah was born. Why had she not manifested the numerals? Where were her numerals?!

An anxious fever rolled across the crowd. What did this mean? They had been delivering their newborns in this same fashion for five years. Would ANY of the children be numbered? Members of the press immediately went to broadcast with news of the failed attempt. Would the Collentacht experiment be a failure? Would any of the Collentacht Pioneer Children have a successful Knowing? Tension was high and the crowd dispersed, but no one knew where to go or what to do.

Meanwhile, Hannah Crockett and her mother were curled up in Hannah's bed sobbing uncontrollably. They had been waiting five years for this day. All the anticipation and planning, preparing Hannah to know her fate and how they would handle the news. All for nothing. The family of three was crushed. Their hopes and dreams for Hannah – destroyed.

13.

Dr. Satania slammed down the phone after he spoke with the Prime Minister. This was a disaster. In order for this project to be a success they needed everything to unfold without a hiccup, and this was a major hiccup. This was more like a big, fat, case of beer drinking, fraternity boy belch. It was a major hit. And the media was running wild with it because it made for great TV. Everyone loved a good crash and burn story. They were going to have a field day with this one. He had to find a way to put the brakes on it. He packed a bag and grabbed his keys. He was headed to Collentacht.

When he arrived in Collentacht the press swarmed his car before he could make it through the front entrance of the lavish gated community. The original builder had included a high brick wall and a heavily fortified gate to keep the riff raff away from his wealthy residents. And while it really wasn't necessary, they had maintained the gated entrance. It gave everything a feeling of authority and glamour. With this latest development, Dr. Satania was wondering if they might have to lock the gate and create a perimeter for safety. It was only a matter of time before the naysayers came knocking on the door to remind him of his past failures and the ethical concerns they loved to shout from the rooftops. Fortunately, they had been a minority so far, but they were a loud and vocal minority. Right now he wanted to be sure to keep them away from the press.

But as he turned the corner into Hannah Crockett's neighborhood he could see he was too late. The kooks and crazies had already arrived. They were everywhere with their picket signs and bull horns, singing songs of humanity and nature, holding hands and demanding that we stop this project. "Stop playing God!" They shouted! "Life happens! Death Happens! Get over it!"

God. Hmph. What a ridiculous notion. There was no God. Their old man in the sky was a joke. When did anyone's God ever do anything for Matthew Santania? He was in control of his own destiny. He didn't need the opiate of religion. He could think for himself.

He continued to roll slowly down the street toward Hannah's home. Local residents were in heated debates on the side of the street with protesters who had made their way into town early that morning. This was exactly what those doubters wanted – to see them fail. Well, he wouldn't allow it. He would save this project, one way or another. He stopped his car in front of Hannah's house and pushed his way through the gawkers. He ignored their microphones and cameras. He put his head down and made his way to the front door. Hannah's father, Bill opened the door to let him in.

The room was filled with all the major players in Collentacht. The medical team that delivered Hannah was seated around the kitchen table. That was his first stop.

"What do you think happened?" he questioned them. "How did we get here?!" His tone got more emphatic, but they just stared back at him. "Dammit!" he slammed his fist on the table. "How did we fail?!" The medical team continued their silence. All morning they had been discussing every moment of that first delivery. They were certain they had followed his orders to perfection. They were confounded. The next baby they delivered would turn five in exactly one week. All they could do was wait.

One week later, Amber Bunting woke up on her fifth birthday with no markings. Her parents were devastated. They'd held out hope that Hannah's misfortune was an isolated case. Now it was looking more unlikely that any of the Collentacht children would bear numerals. At least not the ones delivered by their own medical team. What had they done wrong? What were they missing?

A month went by, and still, every child woke to a bare neck on their fifth birthday. The entire project was swirling in the toilet. Dr. Satania was a laughingstock. Again. He sank into depression.

Then on May 31st, something magical happened. Anthony Lee awoke on his fifth birthday with the numeral 99 on his neck. Wait, how was this possible? None of the other children had been successful patients. How did this one work?

Anthony's mother, Jill, reminded the medical team that Dr. Satania was visiting at the time of Anthony's birth. He arrived at the hospital that morning to meet with the medical team, but he was first on the scene and already had his medical bag at his side, so the nurses asked him if he would be willing to deliver the baby himself. He was thrilled to do so. It had been a while since he'd been in the delivery room. Dakota

Winters was the last time he had delivered a baby and that had been in the lobby of his office building! Now that she mentioned it, the memory was coming back to him. He had totally forgotten that day. There were a few other babies he had delivered since then. They needed to follow those specific children and await the outcome.

This could be good news. Very good news for the project. If children were still manifesting numerals, they simply had to determine what was different about the children he delivered versus the children delivered by the local medical team. That was the key – what was he doing differently that caused the anomaly? He had trained them all to follow his method with the most minute detail. They had displayed the method confidently and he was sure they were sticking to the protocol. So what was different?

And. Then. It. Hit. Him. His medical instruments. He always used the same set of forceps. Even after all these years, he was still using the exact same set of obstetrical forceps that his med school mentor had given him. Every single baby he had delivered was done using those forceps. Perhaps HE was not the common denominator. Perhaps it was the forceps. Could it be that simple? What could be different about his forceps that would cause this entire phenomenon to happen in the first place?

Dr. Satania called each member of the medical team and asked them to meet him at the hospital in one hour. "And bring your medical bag with you. Don't forget your medical bag," he insisted.

They gathered around the table in the staff kitchen, each

with their bag of medical instruments at their side. There was a tray placed in front of each of them.

"Take out your forceps and lay them on the tray in front of you," Dr. Satania instructed. They did as he said. Before them were five sets of obstetrical forceps, all seemingly identical despite the variation in age and brand. Minor differences were evident, but they were all basically the same design. He explained to them that he was beginning to think that it was the forceps, not the doctor, that was causing the biological change in his patients.

"I want us to compare my forceps to the ones you have been using and see if we can find a difference."

They each studied their own set of forceps and then looked carefully at Dr. Satania's forceps. There was a bend in the metal on his that didn't exist on any of the others. It was very subtle. Something you wouldn't really notice unless you were comparing them to others, but there was in fact a distinct difference in the design. Where the others had smooth, flat metal on the blades (they weren't really blades at all, more like scoops, but blade is the technical term for it), his forceps were made with a twist in the metal, but only on one side of the blade. It was difficult to tell if it was a design flaw, or if it was intentional. Dr. Satania had been using them from his first day on the job, so he had not realized his instrument was different in any way. He couldn't imagine that this tiny difference was the cause of the abnormality that caused the Keyall to open and create the markings on these children. Certainly there was more to it than that. But at this point they had no other leads, so it was as likely as anything.

They decided to duplicate the exact design of his forceps and begin using them in the delivery room. It would be five years before they could know for sure if this was indeed the factor that affected the procedure, but they had no other option, so they put the plan into action. A local metal worker was called in to create five identical pairs of forceps that were exact copies of Dr. Satania's pair, twisted blade and all. These would be the instruments used in the delivery of the Pioneer Children.

14.

The years passed slowly with recurrent bouts of disappointment for parents of the children who thought they would be the next generation of Numbered Children. Occasionally a child would wake up with numerals on his or her neck because Dr. Satania had been in town at the time of the birth and had delivered that baby. In all, 12 babies in Collentacht were delivered by Dr. Satania during that first five-year period, and all 12 revealed numerals on their fifth birthday.

The rest of the children in the community were secretly referred to as the Failed Generation. No one ever spoke those words directly to the children, or to their parents, but everyone knew that's what they were – a failed experiment. Dr. Satania was publicly shamed once again, but the dozen children who HAD manifested the numerals were a sign of hope. All was not lost, and the Prime Minister was still very much in support of the project. Granted, he'd left his political role several years back, but his enthusiasm continued with the subsequent administration, and as a now wealthy businessman, the PM continued to support the project with his own funds. Between the government money and private donations from the PM and his inner circle, there was no shortage of funding. The project would continue.

Eventually the second wave of children reached their fifth birthdays. This group had all been delivered using the Satania

Induction Method, but this group also included the new variable of the specially designed forceps. The moment of reckoning was at hand.

Zoie Dinstuhl was the first of this cohort to celebrate her fifth birthday. The community waited anxiously for her to wake that morning to see if her fate would be foretold. Screams of delight came from Zoie's bedroom when she sat up in bed to reveal the numerals five and nine on her neck. And while 59 was not as long as they had hoped, Zoie's parents were thrilled to learn that their child was the first of many success stories of the Pioneer Children. This was very promising.

Over the next few months, several more of the group turned five, and each one woke to their numeric fate. There were some disappointments – two children bore single digit numerals. Never a happy day for the families or the community, but now they knew they had precious little time with their children and could spend it accordingly. It was bittersweet really, but a necessary byproduct of the ability to know one's fate. Sometimes it was going to be less than stellar news. That was the way life worked now. Possessing such knowledge had its risks, but most of the families still agreed it was the right choice for them.

The naysayers were back in full force. Each time a child would experience The Knowing (the revelation of their year of death) the press would run juicy new stories about the protests from those who believed the practice was unnatural and unethical. We weren't meant to possess this kind of information and by doing so, we were playing God. It was far too dangerous the protesters shouted in the streets.

The terms known and unknown had become mainstream now, and neither contained a positive connotation. Nearly every issue in our society was drilled down to a battle between the known and the unknown. There was no in between. You were either for or against The Knowing. Citizens were venomous in their opinions.

When expectant parents chose to take the path of The Knowing they were often met with interrogation and judgment from their own families. The decision had to be made before the child was born since the procedure during childbirth was the means to the end. And once the decision was made, there was no reversing it. At least no way that they knew of yet. So parents were making a lifelong decision for their child before the child was even born. It was a great deal of pressure – the barrage of opinions and commentary didn't make it any easier. It grew so contentious that separate childbirth classes had to be formed for expectant parents who had chosen The Knowing because fights would break out in the classroom. It was an intensely emotional issue for everyone involved. It was changing everything, and there was no going back.

Now that The Knowing was becoming more mainstream, the voices of opposition were getting louder, but the voices of support had one thing in their corner – money. Not only was the former Prime Minister publicly (and financially) supporting The Knowing, but the majority of the wealthy class supported it as well. The option to control one's destiny by knowing how much time they had was appealing in so many ways. The possibilities were endless for ways this knowledge could be used to maximize one's potential for wealth and success. The option wasn't going away, if the wealthy class had any say in the matter, and of course they did.

15.

My name is Kay. They say that I'm one of the lucky ones. Come along and see if you agree.

A few words from the author...
Thank you so much for taking the time to invest in this book project. Remember, if you reply as I ask below, you will get Book 2 for FREE when it is ready.
Now it's YOUR turn to be a part of Book 2.
When you have finished reading Book 1,
I would love to hear your thoughts. Please email me at theknowingmdlima@gmail.com
Here's what I'm hoping to hear from you:

1. How did you hear about the book?
2. Would YOU want to know when you would die?
3. What would you like to see next in the story?
4. How would it change the way you live your life if you did know?

One more thing...
Here's your chance to be a book editor (that would look great on your resume!) If you find any glaring errors in the book, please send a message to the email address above.

A portion of the proceeds from the sale of this book will
be donated to the American Cancer Society's
Making Strides Against Breast Cancer campaign.
If you'd like to donate directly to their vital work to end
cancer as we know it, for everyone, please visit www.mak-
ingstrideswalk.org or https://donate.cancer.org

Dedicated to my amazing family.
No matter how many years we have together,
it will never be enough.
With deepest gratitude to my editor, and dear friend,
Cisa Linxwiler
I have used names of people in my life to name the characters, but the names have absolutely no connection to the persona of the characters they are assigned. I chose them very much at random as I was writing the story, so read nothing into that. Truly.

Dear Reader,

This is not an ordinary book. This is the first piece of a project that you are invited to join. I'd like to thank you for investing in this project – whether that investment be the time you spend reading it, your finances in buying it, or your creative energy in responding to it, sincerely, I thank you.

Book 1 of The Knowing series is intended to lay the foundation for the story and the phenomenon that makes the story possible. It builds the architecture of the narrative, but the deeper narrative and character development are yet to unfold.

Which is where you come in – when you have finished reading Book 1, see the last page for instructions about how to respond. I want YOU to be a part of the story. Share your thoughts and ideas with me. Tell me if you would want to know when you would die, and if so, how would it change the way you live your life? This book project is an interactive experience where you get to help create the story. I hope to weave in as many reader ideas as possible. So, you could see YOUR idea in the next book.

This is unlike any book out there – be a part of it – the adventure, the creation, the unfolding of THE KNOWING.

-M.D. Lima

1.

I must have been about three years old when I first heard the term, The Knowing. Three seems young for such a memory but the recollection is accompanied by the image of my mother's belly swollen with the pending arrival of my little sister, Elizabeth. So I must have been three.

My mother's reaction to the term is what burned the memory into my brain I suppose. She screamed. A shrill howl of utter frustration embroiled with anger and disgust. My mother never screamed. She never even raised her voice. She was a gentle woman who spoke softly and whose touch was even softer than her voice. She was beauty and grace embodied. I adored her. She was my hero.

But that is all I recall. I don't know why she shrieked at the sound of something that is essentially the center of our society. The Knowing. It defines us. We are the Known and the Unknown. That is our way.

It hasn't always been this way. Before The Discovery, no one was Known. My mother believes it was probably better that way. Simpler. More natural. The way life should be. But that's all part of our history now. There is no going back.

The story is told that just a few generations ago, a strange physical manifestation began occurring in five-year-old children of a particular small village. On the morning of their fifth birthdays, the children each developed what appeared to be numerals on the back of their neck, just at the nape. Some children had single digit numerals; others had double. One child even had a triple digit numeral. But he was the only one.

The numerals appeared as though they had been tattooed, but none of the children had done any such thing. No one could explain it, and it had the parents of the village in a frenzy. Was someone terrorizing their children? And how? What did it all mean?

After months of interviews, physical exams, and far more media coverage than they would've preferred, aside from residing in the same village, the one common denominator amongst ALL of the children was that they had been delivered by the same obstetrician. Dr. Matthew Satania.

Dr. Satania, it seems, had a penchant for yanking children from their mother's cervix with a well-worn set of obstetrical forceps. The legend has it that he barely gave the mother a chance to push her baby out before he reached in with his tongs and ripped the child away. In addition to the emotional trauma this undoubtedly caused the parents, the more prominent side effect of this tactic was that with his forceps he had unknowingly (or was it so?) depressed a small section of soft tissue at the base of the child's head, causing each of his deliveries to have the same impression at the back of their skull. Dr. Satania had seemingly created a biological calling card on the body of his patients. It was almost like a small opening, but not quite. More of a dent.

It was from this "dent" that the numerals seemed to flow. As though they had slid right down from the child's brain and onto the back of their neck through that almost like a small opening, but not quite spot.

There were 97 of Dr. Satania's patients in the village who turned five that year. They all bore a numeral. When January of the new year rolled around, parents of then four-year-old Satania patients held their breath in fear. Would their newly turned five-year-olds have the same fate as their predecessors? And what did it all mean? A year had passed, and still, no one could explain anything more than the common factor in Dr. Satania.

January passed and not a single child turning five displayed the numerals. Parents began to relax. This was a good sign. Maybe their children would be untouched by the mysterious mark. Weeks went by, and the world lost interest in the village. Families tried to return to some semblance of normalcy.

Until February 13th. The village broke out in a panic when Rachel Johnson woke up on February 13th, the day of her fifth birthday, with the numeral six on her neck. Her mother let out a wail when Rachel came down the stairs that morning. Rachel broke into such hysteria that she had to be rushed to the hospital and given oxygen. It was three days before her mother could stop crying. She wasn't even certain what she was crying about. But she knew this couldn't be good.

As it turns out, Dr. Satania had been out of the country visiting his family overseas for the entire month of January and the first part of February, five years prior. He didn't deliver any babies in the village during that six-week period. Rachel Johnson was the first delivery he made upon his return to work - February 13th.

2.

By the wee hours of February 14th, the village was under siege. Reporters, government officials, scientists from around the world, and gawkers who wanted to see the Numbered Children, as they called them. By the end of the week, three more children had been numbered, and no one was any closer to understanding why or how this was happening.

Parents would sit anxiously at the bedside of their rising five-year-olds, waiting for their birthday morning sun to rise and reveal their child's fate. Cries could be heard from homes around the village on the morning of many fifth birthdays that year.

Fear ran rampant through the village. Dr. Satania had become a pariah, unable to leave his home. Death threats came in every day as the villagers grew more and more certain that he was to blame for this nightmarish plague on their children. And the longer they went without answers, the more frightened and angrier they became.

Dr. Satania swore that he knew nothing. While he admitted to his proclivity for the use of forceps, he insisted it was because he couldn't bear to see his patients suffer during childbirth, so he hastened the act with a handy set of tongs passed down to him by his med school mentor. He was new to practicing medicine, and very young. The village was his first assignment out of medical school. And though his logic was warped, he seemed sincere and genuinely clueless about the cause of this phenomenon.

Month after month passed with no answers. Dr. Satania closed his practice and returned to his family's home overseas. The threats and the hostility from his community had finally broken him. Government officials insisted he maintain contact with them so they could reach him if any discoveries were made. He agreed and said his goodbyes as he boarded a plane back to his homeland. Perhaps he should've never left home in the first place. Medical school had been such a disaster that this little village is the only place that would hire him. Now he was an exile in his field. He would go home and work in his father's restaurant.

The nightmare continued in his absence. For the next three years, Dr. Satania's babies continued to turn five, and each one continued to bear a numeral marking on his or her neck upon the morning of their fifth birthday. At the end of that third year (five years after the first Numbered Child had been identified), the last of Dr. Satania's Numbered Children turned five on December 31st. The boy woke up with the numeral six on his neck, exactly as Rachel Johnson had done five years prior. It was the first time a single digit numeral had been repeated in more than one child.

That was the first real clue to what would become known as The Discovery. Rachel Johnson, who had manifested the numeral six on her neck, died at the age of six. At the time, no one drew any sort of correlation between the numeral on her neck, and the age of her death. She was tragically killed in a car accident. Her family was too devastated to think of much of anything aside from their grief.

Until Peter Gardener awoke to the same numeral fate. Could it be that simple? Would it be something so morbid? Was the numeral on their neck the age at which they would die? Certainly not. Preposterous. The researchers who had been studying this case since it broke laughed at the very thought. Ridiculous.

Peter Gardener died three months later from a rare form of eye cancer. Only six weeks after he began having severe headaches which were the result of Ocular Melanoma.

Parents of children who bore single digit numerals collapsed into despair. Would their children soon die as well? How could this be? The emotional toll was felt throughout the entire village. Everyone knew a family that was affected by this mystery. No one was untouched.

In the midst of their grief, however, the villagers began to grasp that something good might come from this. With the correlation drawn between the deaths of two Numbered Children, the scientists could now study their remains for more clues. Peter's parents reluctantly agreed to let them study his body. Rachel's family took a great deal of coaxing, but eventually agreed to allow them to unearth her corpse for further study. As agonizing as it was, they hoped the gruesome task might help other families find answers.

3.

Within hours of exhuming Rachel's body, the scientists discovered a biological anomaly in the brains of each of the deceased Numbered Children. Peter's brain was of course much easier to study considering his recent death, but Rachel's corpse was a treasure trove of discoveries despite its decomposition. The clues were still there.

What they found was that the dent made in the child's skull by Dr. Satania's forceps had opened to what appeared to be a tiny cylindrical compartment in the brain. That which felt like a dent from the exterior of the head, was actually more of a tiny lid covering the compartment.

Researchers concluded that the forceps must have broken away a bit of the infant's soft skull tissue during childbirth. Nothing that would be noticeable in an otherwise healthy newborn.

As the child grew it appeared that the soft tissue hardened and healed into place over this area forming a lid. When they removed the lid, a tiny space was revealed – a tube of sorts. It was unlike anything they had seen before in the human brain. A storage compartment that was hidden except for the fact that this deformity created a doorway to the compartment in those children who had been delivered in this manner.

They had what they knew was an important clue, but they had no idea what it meant. Another year passed.

4.

Support groups had formed for the parents of the single digit Numbered Children. Their anxiety was becoming a community issue. It was affecting all facets of village life. They didn't know for sure that their children were soon to die, but the mere suggestion that their numeral might dictate their death age was more than many of these parents could bear. The mental health unit of the village hospital saw a huge uptick in patients suffering from nervous breakdowns. All of them were parents of single-digit Numbered Children. They were cracking from the pressure of anticipating their child's death.

No more children had died, but the next single digit numeral on a Numbered Child was eight, and that child was only seven. The entire village seemed to collectively hold its breath when Chloe Nelson turned eight. Her birthday passed without incident, and everyone breathed a momentary sigh of relief.

In her untamable anxiety, Chloe's mother, Leenie, took every possible precaution to protect her child from any imaginable form of accidental death. Chloe wore any manner of protective gear that her mother could find. The poor child barely left home. Her mother homeschooled her that year to avoid letting her out of her sight.

On the night before her ninth birthday, the village was

bubbling with excitement. If Chloe survived the night, the Numbered Children nightmare might be no more. Maybe the deaths of the first two children were purely coincidental. True, the discovery about their brains was certainly interesting, but that didn't mean all of the children were going to die. They wanted so much for this to be over. Everyone went to sleep that night with hope in their hearts.

In her desperation to protect her child, Chloe's mother crawled into bed beside her so she could keep watch through the night. She fixed her unwavering gaze on her daughter's face like a lion protecting her cub. Her husband awoke to her screams at 1:00 AM when she startled awake to realize she had smothered Chloe in her sleep by inadvertently rolling on top of the child, burying her face in the bed pillows.

Earlier in the evening, having tolerated, but never fully bought into the notion that Chloe was destined to die at age eight, Chloe's father slipped a sleeping pill into his wife's drink at dinner. He had hoped his wife would finally be able to get a bit of rest as she lay next to their precious daughter on this most stressful of all nights. Her anxiety was at maniacal level, and he was afraid she was going to crack from the pressure and lack of sleep.

With the narcotic in her system, Chloe's mother was deeply sedated and never felt or heard a thing. Chloe had slipped away without notice. The coroner judged that she had been dead for approximately two hours. Her death certificate read 11:00 PM. Together, her parents had managed to fulfill her destiny.

The entire village lost its collective mind.

5.

Two more years passed. Every child that had been delivered during Dr. Satania's five-year tenure as an obstetrician had reached their fifth birthday. And every one of them bore a numeral on their neck.

Four more single digit Numbered Children died and two more were nearing what the news media now callously referred to as their "expiration date." None of the single digits had escaped their numeric fate. At this point, it was clear what the numerals meant. But why? And how was it happening?

The years went by and though they never fully fell out of the spotlight, the world grew less interested in the Numbered Children. They went on about their lives, as normally as possible. Many had mental health issues from the strain of knowing when they would die. The anticipation was agonizing and drove several of the now grown children to commit suicide on their fated birthday. Others found solace in drugs and alcohol to numb the constant internal dialogue about their impending date with death. It affected every decision they made. They couldn't escape the gravity of this knowledge. It was too much to carry.

And then there were a few who seemed to embrace the notion that they knew how much time they had and went about their days squeezing life dry of every ounce of joy. Those folks typically ended up with a mountain of debt from their love affair with life (all that high living isn't cheap), but what did they care? They knew they were going to be dead by 29, or 34, or whatever the case may be, so to hell with it. Run up some debt, have a blast and "Sayōnara bitches!"

Fortunately for the credit card companies there were only a few who went down that path. Once they caught on to the scheme, creditors began inquiring about an individual's status as a Numbered Child on the credit application. They wouldn't let that happen again.

Otherwise, the world would mostly forget about that strange Numbered Children story.

Until a Ph.D. student at the village university dug up an article about the phenomenon and decided to write a paper about it. Suddenly, the Numbered Children were causing a stir again.

The student, Olivia Dail, posed a hypothesis that knowing one's time of death would significantly alter the path of one's life. In an effort to prove her hypothesis, she set out to interview the remaining 312 members of the Numbered Children clan. Her ambitious project grabbed the attention of a local reporter, who nudged the story to a national reporter, and suddenly the village was under siege again.

Everyone wanted to return to the scene of the bizarre story about the strangely marked children. Even Dr. Satania (who had not practiced medicine since he went back to his homeland) was dragged in front of a camera. The press tracked him down halfway across the world to interrogate him all these years later.

It was his worst nightmare. He had nearly convinced

himself it was all just a terrible dream. His reality came crashing back as his face again splashed across newspapers and television screens around the world. "Dr. SATAN" they called him. Cartoon images of him with horns and a tail seemed to be everywhere he turned. Someone had even painted a graffiti image of his devilish likeness on the side of his family's home. He was mortified. But there was no escaping it. There was nowhere to hide. They would track him down again. He had to face their cameras and their questions. He packed a bag and boarded a flight to the village.

6.

By the time Dr. Satania (who now preferred to be called Matthew) arrived in the village, emotions were at an all-time high. Villagers were clashing with members of the press who had camped out in every corner of the already bustling town. The few Numbered Children who still lived there (most wanted to get as far away as they could), were being hunted like animals by reporters and freakshow seekers.

Matthew Satania walked into Constable Mark's office and introduced himself. A laughingly unnecessary act considering everyone knew who he was. He was practically a walking, talking ghost story. Children still giggled with delight at scary stories about "Dr. Satan who yanked babies from their mommies!" He read the room and sat down sheepishly in a chair in the corner.

All of the village leaders were gathered in the room. Some looking nervous and fussy, others looking exhausted and strung out. But none of them looked happy. Only a few of those present were old enough to be involved in the original fiasco of the Numbered Children, but everyone knew the story by heart. It had unfortunately become a defining factor of their local history.

No one quite knew how to begin the meeting that seemed to have called itself. Constable Mark, who had in fact been a young officer of the law when this story first unfolded, stood at the front of the room and asked if anyone had any ideas about how they should handle the hysteria at hand.

The room erupted in shouts and hollers, guffaws and laughter. There might have even been a snort or a fart in there somewhere. But no one had a viable answer about how to handle the mania that was just outside the front door of the Great Hall where they met.

Constable Mark shouted for silence in the room. The room settled. "We have to get to the bottom of this craziness," he began. "We have to tell these people something more than the NOTHING we've been telling them all these years! Dr. Satania, I mean, Matthew, have you learned ANYTHING more in all these years that could help us?" His voice was on the edge of pleading as he turned to Matthew.

Matthew stared at his shoes and shook his head. He had put this all behind him years ago. He had tried NOT to think about it. He certainly had not continued researching it.

"Say something, you MONSTER!" came a shout from the back of the room. Matthew sprang to his feet, surprising himself. "I am NOT a MONSTER!" he screamed, tears welling up in his eyes. "I did NOTHING to intentionally hurt anyone. I just want all of this to be over."

"Well, as you can see," Constable Mark pointed to the crowd outside the window overlooking the square, "this isn't going anywhere anytime soon, so I suggest you help us find our way out of it."

With a heavy sigh, Matthew dragged a chair to the giant conference table at the center of the room and motioned for everyone to do the same. After a few moments of shuffling and chairs sliding across the parquet flooring, everyone was seated and at attention.

Matthew bowed his head for a moment, took a deep breath, and said, "Okay, let's begin."

Over the course of several hours that evening, the assembly of men (yes, of course it was a bunch of men) decided to find a way to turn what had been a traumatic past into their finest asset. They had to find a way to push it through the public psyche by making them believe it was a blessing, not a curse. They would set out on the greatest marketing campaign since Christianity. They were going to harness this Numeric Nightmare into a must have fashion statement.

The first order of business was to convince those most deeply affected by this enigma that it wasn't an altogether bad thing. These were the people who had been living this nightmare for years – it wasn't going to be a simple mission. Constable Mark called a meeting of the Numbered Children and their families.

The room was packed wall to wall. Parents, grandparents, siblings, spouses and yes, the Numbered Children themselves, filled the room. There wasn't an empty seat and the tension in the room was stifling. Hundreds of distrusting eyes stared at Constable Mark as he approached the podium.

Constable Mark began by telling the crowd that they all had a remarkable opportunity at hand. He framed the new swarm of attention as a chance to garner support for advanced research into the case of the Numbered Children, and possibly find some sense of closure for all those affected. Distrusting eyes continued to burn through him.

Eternally the wordsmith, Constable Mark wove a tale for his listeners that spoke of vindication for the Numbered Children who had spent much of their lives under the heartless microscope of the media. He even spoke of possible financial reparations for the families affected.

The mention of money had some of the crowd reacting a bit more favorably. Their hardships could certainly stand a bit of financial gain. But he could see that not everyone was so receptive. No amount of money could take away the pain they had endured. So, he changed gears a bit to appeal to their egos.

He talked about how they would all be heroes if scientists could take what they might learn from studying this phenomenon and turn it into some sort of scientific advance rather than a freakshow. The Numbered Children could be pioneers of a new frontier, he crooned. The crowd was not convinced.

A man at the back of the room stood abruptly and stormed out of the assembly hall. The door slammed behind him. The man's wife scurried out after him, tears in her eyes. The couple had recently lost their daughter, Donna, to her numeric providence. Donna was marked with the numeral 27. As fate would have it, she had discovered her pregnancy only days before she was killed by a stray bullet in a drive by shooting. The sting of losing their daughter and unborn granddaughter was simply too much. It was too soon.

Constable Mark cleared his throat nervously and opened his mouth to continue his sales pitch when an older, well-dressed woman stood and shouted over the crowd, "Will we allow all of this to be for nothing? Look at the pain you've all known from carrying this knowledge of their death year...we became so consumed with their death that many of us forgot how to live. This cannot be in vain. My son, Jeremiah, died at 22, just as we knew he would. The first few years of knowing his fate nearly ate us alive. But then we chose to embrace his destiny rather than fear it. And our lives changed in every way. We spent the years we had with Jeremiah LIVING rather than mourning. And it was absolutely magical. I miss him every day, but I am so grateful that I was able to soak up every beautiful moment I had with him. Knowing how much time he had changed everything. We're all going to die. There's no escaping that. But by knowing how long we had together, we spent every day focused on what was truly important to us. We've all heard the phrase, 'Live like you're dying.' Our family actually did that, and it was the greatest gift I have ever received." She straightened her spine and turned to face Constable Mark directly, "I would be willing to allow you to study my son's remains if it will help further the understanding of what we've all been through, and in the hope that something good can come from it for future generations."

The room fell silent. The conviction in her voice was so raw and powerful that even Constable Mark was deeply moved. He realized he had lost himself in her monologue and shook his head to clear his mind and find his way back to the task at hand. As the woman took her seat, Constable Mark uttered only two words, "Thank you." She had just done his job for him.

The next morning, the first thing Constable Mark said to the press was this: "Picture a world where you can plan out every moment of your life…because you know just how many moments you have!"

The room full of reporters was abnormally silent. A few members of the media shifted uncomfortably in their seats and looked around the room to gauge the reaction of their cohorts. No one understood where he was going with this. Was he serious?

Constable Mark continued, painting a picture of a society where people could CHOOSE to find out what year they would die so they could use that information to plan their lives to the moment. "Think of the efficiency, the motivation to live fully, the ability to choose one's path based on one's known finish," he lavished. He painted a picture of a world where uncertainty and worry could be abated because we'd already know how, or at least when, our story ends.

Eyes of distrust turned into looks of curiosity which turned into hushed whispers around the room. They were soaking it up. They were actually discussing it. Albeit quietly and with much guarded voices, but they were discussing it. Constable Mark looked across the room at Matthew, who was taking it all in from the back wall. Matthew's eyebrows raised. Maybe they were onto something.

7.

The next morning a call came in from the Prime Minister's office. Constable Mark nearly choked on his breakfast biscuit when the receptionist buzzed the call through to his phone.

The Prime Minister, it seemed, had been following the story of the Numbered Children since its inception. This new resurgence of the story fascinated him, and he wanted to know more. Constable Mark knew this was his moment. He painted for the Prime Minister the same utopian portrait that he had shared with the press. Prime Minister Blanchman hung on every word. He was hooked.

The concept of knowing one's ultimate finish intrigued the PM both personally and politically. Think of the implications it could have on his ability to support (read: control) the citizenry with this sort of information at his disposal. Resources could be expended more wisely on those who were around for the long haul, with the short termers getting only what they need to survive. Why waste the money on them when we knew they wouldn't be around long? The triple digit numbers could be groomed to maintain the proper world order for years to come. They would be given positions of leadership. Of course, none of this passed through his lips and over the phone line, but his mind raced with possibilities.

As soon as he hung up the phone, Constable Mark called

Matthew to tell him the good news. They were on their way to greatness.

The PM immediately summoned his Health Ministry and discussed the possibility with them, painting the same rosy portrait that Constable Mark had painted for him on the phone. At first the room of doctors and scientists fell silent, just as it did with the press. But much like the members of the media, the room full of health professionals found themselves strangely intrigued. There were a few voices who spoke up with ethical concerns about the prospect, but the snarls and sneers from their peers quieted them quickly. This was not a heroic bunch. The dissenters buried their heads and quickly toed the line. The power that could come from being the nation to launch this scientific bombshell was more enticing than any of them could stand.

And so, it was settled. The Health Ministry would invest a sizable sum into the research of the Numbered Children project in hopes that it would become an amazing prospect for all citizens (and an amazing opportunity for the government to enhance [read: control] the lives of its people). A chance to map out one's entire life with a real sense of purpose from knowing how much time we have. A gift to the people is how they would sell it.

There was just one problem...before they could give that gift they had to figure out how to replicate it.

8.

Constable Mark knew he and Matthew Satania had their work cut out for them. They had to figure out how to dependably recreate the effect. The money rolling in from the health ministry certainly made the task more feasible, but there were so many things that could go wrong. Fortunately, Sandra Zagursky's emotional speech at the recent meeting had inspired others to agree to let the researchers examine the remains of their deceased Numbered Child. The more research samples they could attain, the better chance they had of reverse engineering the numeral effect. So far, they had seven bodies to study, in addition to the two they had researched years before. It was time to get to work.

The seven corpses, in varying degrees of decomposition, were arranged on seven tables across the university laboratory where Matthew had set up his operations. The two original specimens were preserved in the local morgue and would be joining their comrades later that day when the paperwork was complete. They were still awaiting a few signatures from local authorities.

Matthew stood silently at the front of the room staring at the neatly arranged bodies of his former patients. He had once held their newborn bodies in the palm of his hand. And by doing so, he had ruined their lives. Or had he? Maybe this had indeed been a gift. He thought back to Sandra's powerful words...maybe they had lived lives that would never have been possible without the knowledge he had allowed them. With that knowledge better understood and properly harnessed, everyone could live life in absolute fullness. This gift could change the world. He would be a hero. And he would be vindicated. Finally.

He pulled back the sheet on the corpse of Danika Harrison and sliced open the posterior of her skull. For the first time in ages, he smiled. By the end of that day, he had been able to locate the dent, known now as the Keyall, on each of the seven specimens. Each Keyall was identical to the others except one. The Keyall in the brain of Elliott Call had microscopic remnants of a black substance that he had not found in the others. Upon further examination, the remnants were found to be an ink-like substance, much like that found in an octopus. This was a huge break, and though he had been working feverishly for nearly 15 hours, day one had been an enormous success.

Matthew shot up in bed at the sound of his phone ringing just beside his head on the nightstand of his hotel room. The village had only one hotel when he lived here years ago, but thanks to his legacy, the village now boasted 12 hotels to meet the demand of the tourism industry that had been the product of the Numbered Children.

It was Constable Mark. He was breathing heavily. "Come quickly!" he huffed. Matthew could tell Constable Mark was running while he talked. And he wasn't exactly the fittest of the fit. "Lorelei James just dropped dead, and her body is headed to the morgue as we speak. Her family gave us permission to use her remains – you have to get here NOW and begin your exam. You'll probably never have the opportunity to examine a corpse as fresh as this one! Get over here NOW!" Matthew winced at the insensitive nature of Constable Mark's words. "Fresh" was not a word one would ordinarily want to use when referring to a recently deceased human being, but he was right. This was an extraordinary opportunity to examine a body as close to alive as possible (at least for now).

Matthew grabbed his crumpled jeans from the floor, hopped on one foot to dress himself as he crossed the room to reach his shoes and was out the door in moments. When he arrived at the morgue, the technicians had already prepared Lorelei's body on the table for him to examine. She had been dead for just over two hours, so her body was still slightly warm and flaccid, but he didn't have much time. Within the hour she would begin to stiffen and chemical changes in her fibers would begin. He needed to examine her before the Keyall might be altered in some way. He picked up his scalpel and began.

He had only been working for a matter of moments when he gasped and his hands stopped. "Someone bring me a camera, please! Quickly!" One of the technicians handed him the instant camera they had for morgue use and he leaned closely and took several pictures of the area. Suddenly he screamed, "Oh no, what's happening?!" As he stared helplessly, the area he had just photographed began to change. The tiny vein he had examined was shrinking and ultimately disappeared completely. He waited anxiously as the instant film reached full exposure and the photos were revealed. What the images showed, but was no longer visible on Lorelei's corpse was a tiny capillary like vein running from the base of the Keyall down toward the back of the neck. It was the delivery system. The ink substance was released from the Keyall on the 5th birthday (why then? So many questions still to be answered). It travelled down these tiny capillaries to the nape where the ink was dispensed in the form of a numeral.

Matthew grabbed his scalpel and sliced down the back of the neck, peeling back the skin. As the skin pulled away from the tissue beneath, hundreds of tiny veins were revealed that terminated at the dermis layer of her skin. They were spread across the nape of her neck like little pinheads forming a distinct shape. The shape of two numerals. Two and nine. Today was Lorelei's 29th birthday.

A few hours earlier she had been playing football in the backyard with her brothers at her birthday dinner. Her baby brother tripped and careened into her as he went for a catch. The hard hit to her chest caused sudden cardiac death, also known as commotio cordis. She had never had heart problems. She was dead before she hit the ground.

Her family was one of those that had chosen to embrace every moment they had with their precious daughter, and she had made them promise that they would get her body to Dr. Satania immediately so she could help others like her. Her giving heart may have stopped beating, but it had not stopped giving.

To honor Lorelei's wishes, as soon as she was gone their first call was to Constable Mark. In doing so, she had just helped them answer the HOW it was happening. This was the delivery system for the numerals. It was as though the children were being tattooed from the inside with the resulting image showing on the exterior. A superhighway of capillaries that delivered bursts of the ink substance from beneath the skin formed the shape of one, two or three numerals on the nape. In her case, the numerals 2 and 9.

Within seconds of revealing the delivery system, it was gone. Just as the tiny vessel beneath the Keyall had shriveled away, so too did this intricate tangle. Right before their eyes...gone. And they had not photographed it.

"Dammit!" Matthew screamed. "We lost it!"

"Grab a pencil!" Constable Mark yelled. "Everyone, grab a pencil and write down everything you remember about what we saw. Quickly, while it's still new in your minds!"

It sounded crazy, but no one had a better idea, so they did as he said, quietly scribbling and nodding their heads back and forth as if to literally toss the memories around in their brains. When it was clear everyone was finished, they gathered around Lorelei's corpse once again and pulled the sheet over her head, each man clutching the drawing he created from memory.

"This stays in this room!" Constable Mark demanded. "Do you understand me? One damn word leaves this room and I will personally kick your ass!" They were all in shock. In all the years they had known the Constable, they had NEVER heard him swear before. He was a righteous man and very careful to protect his reputation. They all nodded emphatically.

"He's right," Matthew said. "This is very big, but I don't know yet EXACTLY what it means. I need time to study it further. We CANNOT let this information get out. Got it?"

Everyone nodded again and handed their drawings to Matthew. Constable Mark sent them on their way with, "Okay, then. Get out of here. All of you."

When he was sure they were all well gone, he turned back to Matthew. "What does it mean, Matthew?"

"I'm not entirely sure yet," he said with a sly grin, "but I think it's good news...extremely good news. And it's Dr. Satania."

9.

Matthew, or rather, Dr. Satania, didn't sleep a bit that night. He was facing the wee hours of the morning when he got back to his hotel room. Too early to head to the lab on campus and begin working. University Security would get their bloomers in a bind over that. So he sat down at the writing desk and began making notes about what he had seen. He sketched, and scribbled notes, and hashed out ideas and hypotheses. This went on for three hours until the sun came up. Security couldn't balk now. It was officially morning. He would just be an early bird on campus today.

As he turned the corner to head toward his building, he noticed a young woman sitting on the front steps. The sun was barely over the horizon and this woman, this very pregnant woman, had been sitting on the steps of his building for quite some time. She perked up when she saw him in the distance, and tried mightily to get to her feet, but just as she began to rise, she was stricken with pain, and fell back to the steps with a thud. She cried out.

Dr. Satania sprinted across the lawn toward the woman. She was in labor. Freaking hell. This woman was about to have a baby right here on the front steps of Cecil Hall. As he reached the young woman, she cried out again. Freaking hell. Her contractions were getting closer together. She was breathing heavily.

"I want you to," she gasped in pain, "deliver my baby," she gasped again. And then a gush of fluid from between her legs. Her water broke. Freaking hell. Dr. Satania fumbled for his keys to open the building. He had to get her inside. He propped the door open and went to get the now hyperventilating young woman. He tried to talk her through the anxiety and she was able to slow her breathing a bit. He slowly helped her to her feet and they inched their way to the door.

He had no idea he could ever be so happy to see a lobby couch as he was at that moment. He got the woman to the couch and propped her up as best he could. "I'll be right back," he promised the frantic young woman. "I have to get my instruments. I'll be RIGHT BACK!" He tore off down the hall and jammed a key into the door of the office they had given him when he agreed to stay and help with the research. The young woman could hear him tearing apart the room searching for his tools, cursing continuously as he went.

"Yes!" he cried, and he came tearing back down the hallway with a black bag in one hand and a wad of t-shirts under his other arm. He motioned to the t-shirts: "Best I can do in a pinch", there had been a box of t-shirts left in the office closet from its previous occupant. The shirts were all hot pink and read, "Check Your Humps For Lumps" with an image of a camel with breasts in the place of its humps. The young woman tried to smile, but winced in pain instead.

"Yes, of course! Let's get to work!" Dr. Satania knelt down beside the young woman and opened his black medical bag. He packed it into his suitcase when he left his homeland, knowing there was a very real chance he would need it again, but never did he expect it to be so soon.

First, he removed his stethoscope and set it aside. He wouldn't be needing that quite yet. Then he removed the forceps. Yes, THE forceps that he had used all those years before. The very ones that created the cranial deformity that had become the greatest scientific mystery of his time. The young woman saw the forceps, "Please! Take the baby now so we can know how much life he has to live. Make him a Numbered Child!" she begged as she winced again in pain. Her contractions were getting closer and closer. It wouldn't be long now.

The woman grabbed Dr. Satania by the arm, "Will you do it? Will you deliver my baby the way you did all those other children? Please!" He was shocked. He didn't know how to respond. Here was a woman begging him to perform the very procedure that had ruined his life, and that he thought had ruined the lives of all of those poor people. But she WANTED her child to know his numeric fate. She had been sitting on the steps of this building for hours, in labor, waiting for him to arrive so he could intentionally cause a deformity in her child that would predict the year of his death. He stared at her in disbelief. And then he nodded. She fell back onto the couch with a heavy sigh and a bit of temporary relief from the pain. But it was short lived. Her contractions were now three minutes apart. It was time. He lifted his forceps and delivered her baby just as he had done time and again so many years ago. It was, as they say, like riding a bike.

Later that day as Dr. Satania replayed the morning's episode in his mind, he realized he could not have PLANNED a better publicity event. Students and faculty began arriving at the building just moments after he delivered baby boy, Dakota Winters. The press arrived before the ambulance did. Dakota Winters would forever be known as the literal Birthchild of The Discovery, as he was the first infant delivered in the new era of The Discovery.

The young woman, Dakota's mother, was Laurin Winters. She was a member of a group that absolutely boggled Matthew's mind as she described it – they were something like a cult, but maybe more like a colony. Or perhaps it was a full-blown cult. He couldn't be sure, but clearly it was a group of people living in community because they WANTED to number their children. They had already been trying to replicate Satania's technique for the last five years, but had no success. In fact, there had been nineteen babies delivered using failed attempts at his method. Two of the children had severely misshapen heads as a result of the failed attempts. The remaining seventeen seemed to be mostly okay. So far. The first few had reached their fifth birthday with no markings revealed. Their attempts had failed. The community was on the verge of collapse when one of the members saw an article entitled, "The World Returns to the Village of the Numbered Children." They knew this was a sign. This was precisely the boost they needed.

She went on to tell him that there were several women in her group at various stages of pregnancy, all of whom wanted to have their babies using the Satania Induction Method. He had a method? Woah. Wild. He had a cult following. Literally.

This was better than anything he could have ever imagined. He would be able to immediately utilize the technique to deliver these children and begin an entirely new test group of Numbered Children subjects. It would have taken years to get approval for a scientific study like this, and it would have been far too restrictive to achieve the level of saturation he needed to make the Satania Induction Method a go. Satania Induction Method. He liked the way it felt on his tongue and he snorted at himself when he realized how much he was enjoying this new found attention. Admiration, that is. He'd gotten plenty of attention before, but not the kind he wanted. This. This was a damn good feeling, and he wanted more of it.

10.

The decision was made that Constable Mark would maintain their daily administrative operations at the university while Dr. Satania would go with Laurin to meet the members of her community. They called themselves The Unknown. They considered Numbered Children to be The Known. Though they would never be able to know the schedule of their own fate, they wanted it for their children. Very much. So much so that they had all abandoned the conventional lives they were previously living and come together on a plot of land about 20 miles from the village. They wanted to be close to the original Numbered Children village, but not so close that they drew attention to themselves. They feared the government would step in and try to stop them, so they kept their lifestyle hidden. Until now.

With the Health Ministry funding Dr. Satania's new research, and the media gobbling up every word they could find about the possibility of more Numbered Children in the future, they knew this was their time to step into the light. But they were being far too slow about it, in Laurin Winters' opinion, and she didn't have time to wait around on them. She took matters into her own hands and found Dr. Satania for herself. And her plan had unfolded exactly as she'd hoped. Well, aside from the part where she was stuck lying on the cold brick steps of his office for two hours. That was not exactly what she had imagined, but it was a means to an end. And it worked. By golly, it worked. She would have her Numbered Child.

When Laurin and Dr. Satania entered the encampment of The Unknown, a hush fell over the place. Eyes turned to stare at them from every angle, and there was more than one gasp heard around the camp. It was him. THE Dr. Satania was standing before them, and Laurin stood at his side, beaming proudly with her newborn bundle wrapped in her arms. "He did it!" she shouted gleefully. "He delivered baby Dakota, and now he will be a Numbered Child!" She was giddy with delight. The gathered crowd cheered. Some of the women began to weep...many from the joy of the moment...some from sheer jealousy. Their babies had already been born and would never be included among the Numbered Children. As far as was known at the time, there was no other way to initiate the Numbered Child phenomenon other than by using Dr. Satania's method at birth. They would forever carry their bitterness. It was too late for their babies. Two of the mothers were filled with jealous rage. Rather than bearing the numerals of their fate, their babies would forever bear the mark of a failed attempt at becoming a Numbered Child. They were disgraced mothers whose children would be known as the freaks with the misshapen heads. One of the mothers, Christy Moreland, was so furious that she spit on the ground and stormed away. Her absolute indignation erupted in every angry step she took as she disappeared in the direction of her tiny, makeshift home. She would pack up her family and leave the camp the next morning. She wanted no part of this anymore.

Dr. Satania watched her dramatic exit with concern. Dissenters were bad for the cause. He would need to deal with her later. When Christy was no longer in sight, everyone turned back to face Dr. Satania who smiled nervously and thanked them all for their warm welcome, all but Christy Moreland, that is. That one could drop dead for all he cared. In fact, it would be rather helpful if she did. (He would have to tuck away that thought. At least for now. He could revisit it later.)

He was shaken from his thought when he heard, "I'm next!" squealed by a young red head who waddled up to the front of the group with a pregnant belly so engorged that it looked like it would be difficult to breathe. She was ready to pop at any minute. Dr. Satania smiled and extended his hand for her to shake. Instead, she grabbed him and struggled to wrap her arms around him awkwardly for the giant tummy in her way and gave him the closest thing to a hug that she could muster. She squealed again as she took a step back. She was fangirling over an obstetrician. What in the world was going on? He felt like he had tumbled into an alternate universe. Where were the haters and the death threats now? These people worshipped him. He was a god. And this was only the beginning.

When he returned to the village a week later, he had delivered two more babies at the colony of The Unknown and had spent hours teaching the precise details of the Santania Induction Method to the colony's medical team, comprised of four individuals. In their lives before joining The Unknown, two had been doctors, one was formerly a nurse, and one was an EMT. He felt confident that they had studied carefully and were ready to perform the deliveries after he departed. And he was only 20 miles away. He could return if necessary.

A week later he received a call that the medical team had delivered a baby using his technique and they felt confident that this time it was a success. Unfortunately, there was no way to know for sure until the child reached her fifth birthday, but they were hopeful. They had done everything exactly as he had taught them.

By now word had gotten out about the colony of The Unknown, and they were beginning to feel the pressure of the media's presence. Their private compound in the woods was private no more. Reporters reached their remote location by foot, on four wheelers, and one even hovered in a helicopter above. The members of the colony were not amused. Something had to be done.

They called Dr. Satania. His advice was for them to come out of hiding completely and proudly rejoin society. The concept of having the option to be a member of the Numbered Children was gaining more and more popularity. Family members, like Sandra Zagursky, had begun speaking out in support of the procedure and sharing stories of the beautiful life her child was able to lead because they knew how much time they had with him. She, and those like her, sold the idea to society with passion and the kind of emotion only a mother could marshal. Inquiries about becoming a Numbered Child were flooding in every day. It was time for the people of The Unknown colony to step out and sing the praises of the Numbered Children for all the world to hear.

Meanwhile, the original Numbered Children weren't so

sure. The rosy world being painted by officials was hardly the life any of them had lived. Sure, there had been a few out of the bunch who had bucked the norm and lived wild and free. It sounded great. But society would collapse if everyone followed that path.

11.

Spring term had recently ended at the University so students left campus and returned to their home villages for the summer. As a result, the University dormitories were vacant. Dr. Satania, supported by some very strong words of encouragement (read: threats) from Constable Mark, was able to convince the University administration to let the members of The Unknown colony stay in the dorms temporarily. But only temporarily. Students would be back in a few months. The colonists would need to be long gone by that time.

Dr. Satania didn't know what he was going to do with all of these people, but he knew he needed to bring them out where the world could see them. They could be a model community for the Numbered Children project. A living, breathing, model community where he could test best practices and theories and show the world the kind of success they could enjoy if they joined the movement. Yes, he liked that. The movement to help people live their lives with fullness and purpose. Never a moment wasted. Each one accounted for and applied to its finest use for maximum output. They would be a nation of near demigods, controlling their destiny in a way never possible before. His skin prickled at the thought of it. The power. They would be unstoppable. But first he had to figure out what to do with them at the end of the summer. World domination would have to wait for now.

He picked up his phone and dialed the Prime Minister directly. They had become quite chummy through this whole process of creating a new social movement, and Dr. Satania knew he was going to need to call in another favor.

"Blanch," he said rather casually to Prime Minister Blanchman who picked up on the other end of the line. "It's Satan," he and the PM had decided it was comical to refer to Matthew with the very term the world had tried to use to torture him. Now he embraced it. A couple of naughty schoolboys on the playground they were. They both snorted at the sound of the word, Satan. It sent chills of delight down the Prime Minister's spine. It felt so dark and primitive.

"I have to put these cult, I mean, colony people somewhere before the summer is out. I need to find a place for them to set up a proper village and show outsiders what a spectacular future we could have if every child was numbered."

The PM chewed his lower lip, "Hmmmm." Dr Satania could practically hear the PM thinking on the other end of the line. His mind flying through the mountains of political favors he could call in to help them solve this problem. "I know exactly what we'll do," he purred. "There is a district about 150 miles west of here. It's fairly remote. A contractor from the far North came down and started building a housing community for the wealthy. He thought he would make it big by creating a resort type retreat, exclusively for the rich. A lovely idea," the Prime Minister said woefully. "Unfortunately, he ran out of money before it could be finished. It's been sitting there wasting away for over a year. It will need a lot of repair work, and there are quite a few homes that weren't even finished, but it could be a start. We could even come off as social heroes for helping these families find homes AND rebuilding a community in ruin. It's a win – win," he said coyly. "We win, and we win."

And so, it began. The community would be called Collentacht and it would be founded by a group of brave citizens setting out on a new frontier. A new social order. They would go before the rest of us and pave the way for the lives we deserve. The entire world would be watching.

At the announcement of The Unknown colony's departure, the original Numbered Children were relieved. The presence of this new faction was causing more disruption than anyone needed so they were glad to see them go. Until they realized where they were going.

A few of the now grown original Numbered Children were gathered at a coffee shop on the village square chatting about the recent insanity. "Have you seen this Collentacht place where those cult people are going? It's a paradise," said 28-year-old Grant James. Grant had been one of the Numbered Children who had struggled with drug abuse to dull the voices that wouldn't quiet in his head. Life had not been easy for him. He couldn't help but be jealous that this group of "pioneers" was getting the royal treatment when they had been treated like a circus act. He passed around the photo he'd printed from an article online of the now abandoned resort community. "It looks like a run-down heap of junk to me," one of the young women remarked. "Well, it's been sitting there rotting away for a while, but the bones are good. I mean, really, really good. These homes are mini mansions,"

Grant continued. "And some of them not even so mini. I'm barely surviving, and these kids are being handed the keys to the kingdom. It's not right." His voice was bitter from years of feeling like an outcast. The Numbered Children belonged nowhere and to no one. They were outsiders in every way. And now this group of Numbered Children 2.0 were being hailed as pioneers. Heroes even. It made his blood boil. When the photo came back around the table to Grant, he took one more look at the lavish grounds and grandiose homes before he crumpled it into a ball and threw it on the ground with a growl. He wanted HIS piece of the pie.

"Calm down, Grant," Kimberly tried to comfort him. She'd always had a soft spot for Grant. Nothing ever seemed to go his way. He was a sweet guy with terrible luck. "The sooner these people are gone, the better. Who cares where they go?"

"I care," Grant grumbled as he pushed his chair straight back from the table, hopped to his feet and headed straight out the door of the coffee shop. "That dude has got anger issues," quipped one of the guys at the other end of the table. "Leave him alone. He's been through a lot," Kim defended Grant. She always did. "We've ALL been through a lot," the guy mouthed back. She threw a fork at him and stuck out her tongue.

They didn't always get along, but this group of Numbered Children had been through a lot together. And all they had was each other. No one else could understand what life had been like for them. Even their families couldn't truly relate. It was a lot to carry, especially when they were younger. High school had been a horror story for most of them. As if teenage hormones weren't bad enough...throw in the curse of knowing when you were going to die, and it makes for an emotional tidal wave. Especially if you had a low number. The pressure was unbearable. Many of the girls had found ways to conceal their numerals under their long hair or beneath a scarf. It was a bit harder for the guys to hide their marking with their shorter haircuts and low collars. It was there for everyone to see. And no one ever let them forget. It was always very clear that the Numbered Children were outsiders. No one wanted anything to do with those freakshow kids. They were cursed, and no one wanted to take the chance that the curse was contagious. The fact that the new kids were going to be treated like celebrities was maddening, even for those who didn't outwardly admit it. Their lives had been so unfair. Many of them wondered why would anyone WANT this life for their children? It made no sense at all.

12.

As soon as their travel arrangements were made, The Unknown colony members were anxious to pack their things and make a new start in Collentacht. They knew nothing about their new home, but the last few years had been difficult living rough in their hidden woodland encampment, and even these last few months of piling into university dorms had been less than comfortable. They were looking forward to living in real houses again. They had been in hiding for far too long. Some of the youngest children who had been born at the encampment had never seen indoor plumbing or heat until they arrived at the University dorms. They would be fascinated with the notion of having an entire home of their very own. And now that Dr. Satania had instructed them on how to properly perform his delivery technique, they would surely be reaping the rewards of their die-hard commitment to this movement.

The years passed as the Collentacht community was rebuilt and ultimately became a highly sought after destination. Residents maintained gorgeous homes on perfectly manicured lawns and the area offered luxurious accommodations to those who wanted to escape to the oasis for the weekend or a bit longer. Out-of-town visitors were often more interested in sightseeing the local residents, who had become well known all over the world for the social experiment at which they were the center, than they ever were of the local sights. An entire village of people who had rejected normal society and instead chosen to pursue a completely new order of things – it was fascinating. But there was no denying that the local sights were truly luxurious, and the Collentacht community was nicer than any community built for the rest of the citizenry. And people were starting to talk.

Dakota Winters was now four years old. He would be the first of the Collentacht Numbered Children, now known as the Pioneer Children. The PM felt like the former nomenclature wasn't as flattering as he would like. They needed to have a name that brought hope for the future. The members of the cult formerly known as The Unknown had embraced the new name, but still used the terms known and unknown to differentiate between those who would be marked and those who were not.

Dakota would turn five in two weeks. The Collentacht community could barely stand the wait. They prepared for his day as though he was about to be coronated. He was the embodiment of everything they believed – knowing the approximate date of the end of one's life would change everything about how they lived that life. They would command their own destiny.

The morning of Dakota's fifth birthday arrived. There were throngs of people waiting on the street in front of the Winters home that morning before the sun came up. Even the press had come in for the occasion. Everyone wanted to know how long the first Pioneer Child would have. Would he be a single digit? Would he be around for another century with a triple digit? The wait was nearly over.

Dakota's mother, Laurin, the feisty young woman who had labored on the office building steps for hours waiting for Dr. Satania to arrive that fateful day five years ago, had barely slept a wink all night. Her child was the first of a new generation. She beamed with pride as she tiptoed into his room, just before sunrise.

"Good morning, precious boy," she whispered softly into his tiny ear. "Rise and shine birthday boy." At that, his eyes popped open, and he sat upright.

"What is it? Tell me momma! What's my numeral?" Even at such a young age, Dakota knew this was a big day. He didn't fully understand what it meant that today was the day of his Knowing but everyone seemed very excited, so he was as well.

His mother brushed his hair away from his neck and pulled down the collar of his pajama shirt.

88.

Her baby was going to live a good, long life. Tears welled up in her eyes.

"What is it?" he demanded. "What does it say?" He was sounding panicky at her silence, so she gathered herself and said, "88 my sweet boy. It says 88."

"What does it mean?" he begged her for more. He wanted to understand.

"It means you are going to live a very long life. We have lots of time together."

Dakota smiled at the thought of many years with his mother. He loved her and wanted to stay with her forever.

As the sun came over the horizon, the crowd outside started to grow impatient.

"Come out and show us!" they cried from the street.

Dakota hopped out of bed. He knew they were waiting for him. He felt like a superhero. He ran to the front door. Laurin hurried along behind him. Laurin wrapped her robe tightly around her and opened the front door. The crowd on the street cheered at the sight of the young boy and his mother.

She pushed open the glass storm door and they stepped out onto the front porch.

"Tell us, already!" came a voice from the crowd. They were anxious and impatient. This was such a big day.

Laurin wrapped her arm around her child and they stepped forward a bit, she nudged Dakota to turn around and she lifted his hair from his neck.

"88," she yelled to the crowd trying to speak above the noise as she revealed his markings. There was a split second of silence as they processed what she had told them and then the crowd erupted in hoops and hollers, screams and cries.

88! He would live a long life! This was wonderful news. Just as they had hoped.

Over the next week, the two additional babies that Dr. Satania had delivered for them turned five and each displayed numerals, just as they'd hoped. Timothy Griffin woke to a 67 and Savannah Grey bore the numeral 102. Timothy would have a respectable length of time – he could have a good life. Savannah would be tapped for leadership. Anyone who would be around that long would need to be carefully groomed to maintain our societal order, as it should be.

There were now three Known children in the Collentacht community. Excitement was growing. In just over a week, the next Pioneer Child would turn five. Hannah Crockett was the first baby the community's small medical team had delivered on their own after learning the proper technique from Dr. Satania. Her Knowing would be another step in the right direction toward a new societal norm.

When the day arrived, the scene was repeated on the street in front of the Crockett home. The crowd waited as the sun rose, but no one came through the front door. They waited a few more minutes, chatting and speculating. This went on for nearly an hour when the front door finally opened. The crowd cheered, just as they had done when Dakota emerged only weeks before. But Hannah was not there. And neither was her mother. Instead, Hannah's father, Bill Crockett, stepped onto the porch. His body language did not read celebration.

"There is no marking," he said to the crowd. His voice broke as he continued, "Hannah is not a member of the Pioneer Children. Her Knowing has been a failure."

The energy of the crowd deflated in an instant. What was he saying? How could this be? They had done exactly as Dr. Satania had taught them when Hannah was born. Why had she not manifested the numerals? Where were her numerals?!

An anxious fever rolled across the crowd. What did this mean? They had been delivering their newborns in this same fashion for five years. Would ANY of the children be numbered? Members of the press immediately went to broadcast with news of the failed attempt. Would the Collentacht experiment be a failure? Would any of the Collentacht Pioneer Children have a successful Knowing? Tension was high and the crowd dispersed, but no one knew where to go or what to do.

Meanwhile, Hannah Crockett and her mother were curled up in Hannah's bed sobbing uncontrollably. They had been waiting five years for this day. All the anticipation and planning, preparing Hannah to know her fate and how they would handle the news. All for nothing. The family of three was crushed. Their hopes and dreams for Hannah – destroyed.

13.

Dr. Satania slammed down the phone after he spoke with the Prime Minister. This was a disaster. In order for this project to be a success they needed everything to unfold without a hiccup, and this was a major hiccup. This was more like a big, fat, case of beer drinking, fraternity boy belch. It was a major hit. And the media was running wild with it because it made for great TV. Everyone loved a good crash and burn story. They were going to have a field day with this one. He had to find a way to put the brakes on it. He packed a bag and grabbed his keys. He was headed to Collentacht.

When he arrived in Collentacht the press swarmed his car before he could make it through the front entrance of the lavish gated community. The original builder had included a high brick wall and a heavily fortified gate to keep the riff raff away from his wealthy residents. And while it really wasn't necessary, they had maintained the gated entrance. It gave everything a feeling of authority and glamour. With this latest development, Dr. Satania was wondering if they might have to lock the gate and create a perimeter for safety. It was only a matter of time before the naysayers came knocking on the door to remind him of his past failures and the ethical concerns they loved to shout from the rooftops. Fortunately, they had been a minority so far, but they were a loud and vocal minority. Right now he wanted to be sure to keep them away from the press.

But as he turned the corner into Hannah Crockett's neighborhood he could see he was too late. The kooks and crazies had already arrived. They were everywhere with their picket signs and bull horns, singing songs of humanity and nature, holding hands and demanding that we stop this project. "Stop playing God!" They shouted! "Life happens! Death Happens! Get over it!"

God. Hmph. What a ridiculous notion. There was no God. Their old man in the sky was a joke. When did anyone's God ever do anything for Matthew Santania? He was in control of his own destiny. He didn't need the opiate of religion. He could think for himself.

He continued to roll slowly down the street toward Hannah's home. Local residents were in heated debates on the side of the street with protesters who had made their way into town early that morning. This was exactly what those doubters wanted – to see them fail. Well, he wouldn't allow it. He would save this project, one way or another. He stopped his car in front of Hannah's house and pushed his way through the gawkers. He ignored their microphones and cameras. He put his head down and made his way to the front door. Hannah's father, Bill opened the door to let him in.

The room was filled with all the major players in Collentacht. The medical team that delivered Hannah was seated around the kitchen table. That was his first stop.

"What do you think happened?" he questioned them. "How did we get here?!" His tone got more emphatic, but they just stared back at him. "Dammit!" he slammed his fist on the table. "How did we fail?!" The medical team continued their silence. All morning they had been discussing every moment of that first delivery. They were certain they had followed his orders to perfection. They were confounded. The next baby they delivered would turn five in exactly one week. All they could do was wait.

One week later, Amber Bunting woke up on her fifth birthday with no markings. Her parents were devastated. They'd held out hope that Hannah's misfortune was an isolated case. Now it was looking more unlikely that any of the Collentacht children would bear numerals. At least not the ones delivered by their own medical team. What had they done wrong? What were they missing?

A month went by, and still, every child woke to a bare neck on their fifth birthday. The entire project was swirling in the toilet. Dr. Satania was a laughingstock. Again. He sank into depression.

Then on May 31st, something magical happened. Anthony Lee awoke on his fifth birthday with the numeral 99 on his neck. Wait, how was this possible? None of the other children had been successful patients. How did this one work?

Anthony's mother, Jill, reminded the medical team that Dr. Satania was visiting at the time of Anthony's birth. He arrived at the hospital that morning to meet with the medical team, but he was first on the scene and already had his medical bag at his side, so the nurses asked him if he would be willing to deliver the baby himself. He was thrilled to do so. It had been a while since he'd been in the delivery room. Dakota

Winters was the last time he had delivered a baby and that had been in the lobby of his office building! Now that she mentioned it, the memory was coming back to him. He had totally forgotten that day. There were a few other babies he had delivered since then. They needed to follow those specific children and await the outcome.

This could be good news. Very good news for the project. If children were still manifesting numerals, they simply had to determine what was different about the children he delivered versus the children delivered by the local medical team. That was the key – what was he doing differently that caused the anomaly? He had trained them all to follow his method with the most minute detail. They had displayed the method confidently and he was sure they were sticking to the protocol. So what was different?

And. Then. It. Hit. Him. His medical instruments. He always used the same set of forceps. Even after all these years, he was still using the exact same set of obstetrical forceps that his med school mentor had given him. Every single baby he had delivered was done using those forceps. Perhaps HE was not the common denominator. Perhaps it was the forceps. Could it be that simple? What could be different about his forceps that would cause this entire phenomenon to happen in the first place?

Dr. Satania called each member of the medical team and asked them to meet him at the hospital in one hour. "And bring your medical bag with you. Don't forget your medical bag," he insisted.

They gathered around the table in the staff kitchen, each

with their bag of medical instruments at their side. There was a tray placed in front of each of them.

"Take out your forceps and lay them on the tray in front of you," Dr. Satania instructed. They did as he said. Before them were five sets of obstetrical forceps, all seemingly identical despite the variation in age and brand. Minor differences were evident, but they were all basically the same design. He explained to them that he was beginning to think that it was the forceps, not the doctor, that was causing the biological change in his patients.

"I want us to compare my forceps to the ones you have been using and see if we can find a difference."

They each studied their own set of forceps and then looked carefully at Dr. Satania's forceps. There was a bend in the metal on his that didn't exist on any of the others. It was very subtle. Something you wouldn't really notice unless you were comparing them to others, but there was in fact a distinct difference in the design. Where the others had smooth, flat metal on the blades (they weren't really blades at all, more like scoops, but blade is the technical term for it), his forceps were made with a twist in the metal, but only on one side of the blade. It was difficult to tell if it was a design flaw, or if it was intentional. Dr. Satania had been using them from his first day on the job, so he had not realized his instrument was different in any way. He couldn't imagine that this tiny difference was the cause of the abnormality that caused the Keyall to open and create the markings on these children. Certainly there was more to it than that. But at this point they had no other leads, so it was as likely as anything.

They decided to duplicate the exact design of his forceps and begin using them in the delivery room. It would be five years before they could know for sure if this was indeed the factor that affected the procedure, but they had no other option, so they put the plan into action. A local metal worker was called in to create five identical pairs of forceps that were exact copies of Dr. Satania's pair, twisted blade and all. These would be the instruments used in the delivery of the Pioneer Children.

14.

The years passed slowly with recurrent bouts of disappointment for parents of the children who thought they would be the next generation of Numbered Children. Occasionally a child would wake up with numerals on his or her neck because Dr. Satania had been in town at the time of the birth and had delivered that baby. In all, 12 babies in Collentacht were delivered by Dr. Satania during that first five-year period, and all 12 revealed numerals on their fifth birthday.

The rest of the children in the community were secretly referred to as the Failed Generation. No one ever spoke those words directly to the children, or to their parents, but everyone knew that's what they were – a failed experiment. Dr. Satania was publicly shamed once again, but the dozen children who HAD manifested the numerals were a sign of hope. All was not lost, and the Prime Minister was still very much in support of the project. Granted, he'd left his political role several years back, but his enthusiasm continued with the subsequent administration, and as a now wealthy businessman, the PM continued to support the project with his own funds. Between the government money and private donations from the PM and his inner circle, there was no shortage of funding. The project would continue.

Eventually the second wave of children reached their fifth birthdays. This group had all been delivered using the Satania

Induction Method, but this group also included the new variable of the specially designed forceps. The moment of reckoning was at hand.

Zoie Dinstuhl was the first of this cohort to celebrate her fifth birthday. The community waited anxiously for her to wake that morning to see if her fate would be foretold. Screams of delight came from Zoie's bedroom when she sat up in bed to reveal the numerals five and nine on her neck. And while 59 was not as long as they had hoped, Zoie's parents were thrilled to learn that their child was the first of many success stories of the Pioneer Children. This was very promising.

Over the next few months, several more of the group turned five, and each one woke to their numeric fate. There were some disappointments – two children bore single digit numerals. Never a happy day for the families or the community, but now they knew they had precious little time with their children and could spend it accordingly. It was bittersweet really, but a necessary byproduct of the ability to know one's fate. Sometimes it was going to be less than stellar news. That was the way life worked now. Possessing such knowledge had its risks, but most of the families still agreed it was the right choice for them.

The naysayers were back in full force. Each time a child would experience The Knowing (the revelation of their year of death) the press would run juicy new stories about the protests from those who believed the practice was unnatural and unethical. We weren't meant to possess this kind of information and by doing so, we were playing God. It was far too dangerous the protesters shouted in the streets.

The terms known and unknown had become mainstream now, and neither contained a positive connotation. Nearly every issue in our society was drilled down to a battle between the known and the unknown. There was no in between. You were either for or against The Knowing. Citizens were venomous in their opinions.

When expectant parents chose to take the path of The Knowing they were often met with interrogation and judgment from their own families. The decision had to be made before the child was born since the procedure during childbirth was the means to the end. And once the decision was made, there was no reversing it. At least no way that they knew of yet. So parents were making a lifelong decision for their child before the child was even born. It was a great deal of pressure - the barrage of opinions and commentary didn't make it any easier. It grew so contentious that separate childbirth classes had to be formed for expectant parents who had chosen The Knowing because fights would break out in the classroom. It was an intensely emotional issue for everyone involved. It was changing everything, and there was no going back.

Now that The Knowing was becoming more mainstream, the voices of opposition were getting louder, but the voices of support had one thing in their corner – money. Not only was the former Prime Minister publicly (and financially) supporting The Knowing, but the majority of the wealthy class supported it as well. The option to control one's destiny by knowing how much time they had was appealing in so many ways. The possibilities were endless for ways this knowledge could be used to maximize one's potential for wealth and success. The option wasn't going away, if the wealthy class had any say in the matter, and of course they did.

15.

My name is Kay. They say that I'm one of the lucky ones. Come along and see if you agree.

A few words from the author...
Thank you so much for taking the time to invest in this book project.
Now it's YOUR turn to be a part of Book 2.
When you have finished reading Book 1,
I would love to hear your thoughts. Please email me at theknowingmdlima@gmail.com
Here's what I'm hoping to hear from you:

1. How did you hear about the book?
2. Would YOU want to know when you would die?
3. What would you like to see next in the story?
4. How would it change the way you live your life if you did know?

One more thing...
Here's your chance to be a book editor (that would look great on your resume!) If you find any glaring errors in the book, please send a message to the email address above.